I0700666

HANG TIME

Stories

Brendan Gillen

.406 Press

© Brendan Gillen, 2025
All rights reserved.

No part of this publication may be reproduced, distributed, or transmitted in any form or by any means, including photocopying, recording, or other electronic or mechanical methods, without the prior written permission of the publisher, except as permitted by U.S. copyright law.

The story, all names, characters, and incidents portrayed in this production are fictitious. No identification with actual persons (living or deceased), places, buildings, and products is intended or should be inferred.

ISBN 978-1-967135-03-5

Cover Photo by Brendan Gillen
Cover Design by Jared Hedges

.406 Press | www.406press.com

"You have to keep running. I always believed I was going to be safe."
— Rickey Henderson

Stories

Headhunter

Sometimes I have this dream that I'm in the Bigs, on deck, forty-thousand breathing fire, and our second baseman, a speedster with the Delino DeShields double-earflap, has just grounded out to first. My walk-up music begins to chime from the heavens and it's not "Thunderstruck" or "Ambitionz Az A Ridah" or "Shook Ones," no, it's "Jesus Was a Cross Maker" by Judee Sill, because what is hitting a baseball if not a miracle, and I carry my bat over my shoulder like it weighs a ton. The home crowd is baffled: what is this song, what is this shimmering resonance? Is it religious? Is it cosmological? Is it a spell? But there's enough of a countrified shuffle to get even the skeptics moving, and suddenly everyone knows the words—*A bandit and a heartbreaker*—and as the chorus rains down, I dig into the batter's box, coolly raising my hand for Time like I know precisely how all of this is going to end. I spit into the dirt, the mark of a true hard-ass, but my phlegm is all busted, too thick, too red, a pool of copper on my tongue, a rusty sludge at my cleats, and when I look up at the pitcher, I can tell by his crooked smirk he's got a blade tucked in his glove. He nods, pitch selected, and this is the part where even in my dream I know I'm staring down a night terror, the kind that only ends in a thunderclap headache, the kind that jolts me awake in a stew of sweat, the kind of white-hot brain burn that makes my nose run and my eyes water and swear I'm about to die for the thousandth time, the kind that can turn you into a Believer. But before all that, before I'm reminded that pain is a long game and acceptance is hard-won, the music turns warbled and viscous like somebody pulled the plug on a turntable. The pitcher begins his windup, a high-legged twist of limber violence, a headhunter with a knife in his fist, and instead of parking my weight on my back-leg, instead of squashing the bug, instead, even, of squaring to bunt, I lay my bat in the dirt and get down on my knees and hear a collective gasp cascade the horseshoe fortress as I close my eyes and silently begin to pray.

Lunchbreak

There was a bear in the woods where Davis snuck out for his lunchbreak. First time he saw it scared the piss out of him. He was sitting on a rotted log having his roast beef and Coke and listening to the Reds get walloped when he heard a thick rustle in the overgrowth about fifty yards away, just past the stream that was all but cracked earth. He half expected to see Ellis pop his ruddy boyish face from behind a tree and say *Gotcha* or some shit, then fire his ass on the spot.

The bear was the size of a fridge. Lumbering on all fours. Davis could see the musculature at work beneath all that black fur, could hear the labored exhalations that were somehow profoundly relatable. That seemed to say: *Is this all there is?* The bear hadn't spotted him. Or if it had, it didn't seem to care. Hell, Davis hardly cared himself. Hardly knew how he got here. Not Middletown. Not the body shop. Not even the divorce from Grace. No. The question that gripped his throat with bony fingers was: who was he anymore? His life was half over. Moreso probably. He hadn't seen Millie since she blew out the candles on her fourth birthday. He hated his job. Ellis. His car. The Reds for how they always broke his heart. The click in his shoulder that reminded him of the injury that snatched away his fastball just as the scouts came knocking. Was there a road ahead for a man like him? Did he have the energy to find out? Hell, what he did know was you were supposed to avoid eye contact, hold your breath, play some version of dead. Sort of like how he acted around Ellis at the body shop.

Eventually, the bear decided there wasn't much of interest, made an about-face, and vanished into the woods. Davis felt a heavy sadness in its absence. So, he left a gift. He unwrapped the rest of his sandwich, set it down where he sat, clicked off the game, and made his way back to work.

He returned the next day. And the next. Each time closing the gap. And if things took a vicious turn? So be it.

There was no schedule or pattern. The bear showed up when it felt like it. But each time it came closer and closer, by now well fed on roast beef and tomato and horseradish on white. Maybe, Davis thought, it needed the company too.

One morning, Ellis dressed him down in front of a customer, a good-looking young woman who'd come in with a blue Cherokee. Davis had used an aftermarket catalytic converter to save money, just like he'd been asked to do since Ellis had taken over the shop from his father. And now here he was, emasculated by the spoiled little shit trying to get laid. "Apologies, ma'am," Ellis was saying, "I've told Davis here that the one thing we never do at Ellis Auto is cut corners. Need to get them old ears checked, don't you, Davis?"

Davis fumed in silence and decided he wouldn't come back from lunch until he fed the bear by hand. Until he got as close as possible. Felt its heavy breath on his skin. Proximity to a raw force that had the power to destroy him. That could shake him awake from the stupor of his life. He hoped the bear had come to understand his intentions. That he came in the name of peace and companionship. And if it didn't? Well, then he'd chalk it up to a rift in the order of things that had nothing to do with his existence. Not that he'd be around anymore to hash it all out.

The bear was already there when he ambled down, its shiny coat striated by the skeletal shade of an oak that had all but shed its leaves.

"Hey there, boss man," Davis said, almost a whisper.

The bear looked him dead in the face, eyes that were galaxies of absence. Davis shivered. The bear looked lazily away and suddenly Davis felt very silly, felt tears begin to chase him down. But before they salted his cheek, the bear looked at him once more and began to paw its way over.

"You a hungry dude?" Davis said. He wiped his nose on his sleeve, dug excitedly in his rucksack for his lunch. "Brought extra today."

The bear stopped a few feet away. But Davis could feel the magnetism. The hairs of his neck stood at attention. A cold drop of sweat trickled down his flank beneath his coveralls.

"All for you," Davis said. "Come eat." He unwrapped one sandwich, then the other, offering them with open palms like some sort of sacrament.

The bear drew closer and closer still. It blinked and Davis could see the film of its eyes. The long curl of the claws, shockingly white. And the smell, a deep, earthy musk that reminded Davis of river muck.

"I appreciate you," Davis said, in the lilting tone he had once used with Millie when she was an infant. He had stopped short of saying *love* but resolved that if he ever saw his daughter again, he would say it over and over.

The bear sighed.

Davis stifled a giggle, felt giddiness well up in his chest. He held out the sandwiches, felt the hot puffs of air from the wet black nose, nostrils that expanded and contracted with a rhythm of their own.

When Davis felt the first bite, he pictured himself as a boy, an only child, about the age Millie was now, lonely, but hopeful. The bike rides he would take after school let out, but before baseball practice, up to the steep hill where the oaks thinned to a clearing. He would crest the hill and count backwards from ten, imagining the ballplayer he would become, the life he'd lead. Then he would shove off, the sharp incline drawing him down and down, faster and faster, and he would lift his feet from the pedals and say his prayers, terrified and wild and free.

Invaders

Pace swung his wedge and took a chunk out of the fairway. The ball dropped well short of the pin, which was about seventy yards away.

"Golf's supposed to be nonviolent," Phillips said.

Pace shook his white-gloved hand near his crotch, bent down to retrieve the patch of turf to tamp it into the gash he'd created, noticed a pale flash in the dirt.

"Some clown buried his ball," he said. He crouched down and dug at the moist Florida earth. "Jesus fuck."

Phillips came over and looked down at what Pace had found.

"A dang burial ground," Phillips said, took off his UF visor, wiped his brow.

"What you think it is?"

"Some bad juju, that's what it is."

"Naw, it's not like that," Pace said. He scooped dirt away from the skull and lifted it free. It was starch white with fine fissures spidering the cranium. It fit comfortably in the palm of his hand. The bottom jaw was missing.

"Bro, you better ditch that," Phillips said.

"You think it's an iguana?" Pace said, turning the skull in his hands. He was struck by how light it was, the gaping eye holes. A tiny dinosaur.

"Telling you, you're inviting malevolence. Saw it on a show."

"Bet it's an iguana," Pace said. He held it up to his ear.

"You losing it?" Phillips' voice wavered. "Can't have you losing it."

Hell, maybe he was losing it. But there was something soothing about the soft and dense pocket of air created by the rigid cavity of the skull against his own.

He stood up and brought the skull to his golf bag which leaned on its kickstand in the rough. He unclipped his towel and wrapped the skull in it, zipped it away in a side pouch.

"You're keeping that shit?" Phillips said. He looked at Pace with alarm.

"Could be lucky."

"Or the flip."

"You believe in that?"

"More than I believe in luck."

And Phillips was right. Pace shot like shit the rest of the round, sprayed balls all over the course, lost a full sleeve in the water on sixteen. But he chalked it up to being distracted, pulled by a desire to hold the skull, study it, for what he didn't know.

In the parking lot after the round, Pace handed Phillips the fifty bucks they'd put on the game and didn't even bother changing out of his spikes.

"Guess that means no chicken poppers," Phillips said.

"Not this time," Pace said, closing his clubs in the trunk. "Got something I gotta take care of."

Phillips sucked his teeth and Pace could tell Phillips, in his own way, was concerned about him, but didn't have the vocabulary to express it. When Pace's fiancée left him for her thesis advisor, the closest they came to discussing matters of the heart was when Phillips took him out to get loaded and put his card down when the bill came.

"My advice?" he'd said, clamping a hand on Pace's shoulder. The edges of his words were blurry with drink. "Get laid. Helps the confidence."

But that was nine months ago, and Pace still hadn't gotten laid. Not because he didn't want to, but because he still felt it would betray Cassie somehow, despite the fact she had been the one to betray him.

He could tell none of this to Phillips of course. So as he started up his car, he rolled down the window and raised a middle finger.

"Next time I'm going to smoke your ass," he said.

He needed a place to put it. His place had no mantle. There was only one bookshelf. Someplace central, so he could spot it easily. He was a collector, the impulse to preserve stories. Records and books cluttered his bungalow, stacks on the floor, toppled over in corners. The compulsion had grown stronger since he'd been on his own. It was easy to say he was trying to fill a hole, something fundamentally absent within himself. But it was bigger than that. Pace knew, that on some level, surrounding himself with objects was a way of fending off death, a fortress of preservation. In the end, the objects would outlast him, but, he figured, it couldn't hurt to layer himself in impermanence.

He placed the skull atop his microwave beside a shaker of red pepper flakes and a bear-shaped bottle of honey. He marveled at how aerodynamic it was, the tapering snout, the delicate lattice of bones that made up the eye sockets. The row of little teeth, almost entirely intact, save for a few gaps along the top left jaw.

Iguanas were considered invasive in the area. Friends of his that owned homes bragged of picking them out of trees with high-powered BB guns. They would send him photos of brilliant green lizards laid out dead on a deck chair. The images made him feel vaguely ill. *You guys are fucking with the ecosystem,* he would tell them. *Well those bastards are fucking with my pH balance,* they would say. *My pool is practically green with their shit.* Then, with a rubbery accent like Scarface, *I leave one dead on the diving board as a warning to his fam-i-ly.*

Pace began speaking to it. At first, he hardly noticed he was doing it at all. He would be in the kitchen, dicing a sweet potato, when he would realize he'd been having a full-on conversation with three-quarters of an iguana skull. The kinds of things he'd say to Cassie if he ran into her at Ikea. He'd been a *good catch*? What the fuck did *that* mean? And how did it feel, really, to be so selfish? The answers came to him not in Cassie's reedy tang, but in a voice altogether smokier, sexier, one that seemed to insinuate he would always and forever be alone. The one question he could never work up the nerve to ask the skull was how long ago she'd stopped loving him.

Getting rid of it never occurred to him, even after he'd turned down several invitations to win his money back from Phillips, double or nothing.

"The fuck you doing inside all day?" Phillips said to him after one such exchange on the phone.

"Sorting things out," Pace said. He looked at the skull as he spoke, winked at it.

"You got me worried, bub," Phillips said. There it was. "Stories like this end with colorless fumes in a garage."

"The only thing you need to worry about is your short game," Pace replied.

"Just trash the fucking thing," Phillips said, and hung up.

There was a difference between solitude and loneliness, Pace knew. The tricky part was treading the line. Cassie always gave him a hard time for not going out more with her and her friends from grad school.

"You're turning into a hermit," she'd told him once, touching up her eyelashes in her dresser mirror. By then she hardly looked at him.

What he never let on to was the depths of his social anxiety. The hum that seemed to course beneath the surface of his skin. You couldn't be rejected if you never gave yourself the chance to make a fool of yourself.

One day, a month or so after he'd found the skull, he came home from the office to find it missing. Gone. It was no use searching his bungalow; he'd never once moved it from its place atop the microwave. He nearly had a panic attack, clutched his chest and slid to the kitchen floor. When he caught his breath, he went into his bathroom. Sure enough: Phillips had forgotten to close the window.

He sped right over, parked in the driveway behind Phillips' yellow Jeep. He popped his trunk, retrieved his three-wood, the lightest club he owned. He marched up the walkway, pressed the button, heard the hollow chime within. Everyone seemed to think they knew what was best for him. All he wanted now was to be left alone. Was that so fucking hard?

He was startled when Angela answered the door cradling their newborn. She grinned at him wide-eyed, as if he was holding a giant check, and he felt like a fool.

"So good to see you!" she said, and leaned in. He had no choice but to kiss her cheek. She clocked the club in his hand and whispered conspiratorially: "I'll go get him. He won't shut up about how much he misses playing with you."

She disappeared inside and Pace had to swallow the lump in his throat. He retreated down the walkway and got into his car without looking back. He reversed down the driveway and without much in the way of conscious thought, found himself on the way to the driving range. It was time to get back into playing shape.

Big Phipps Climbs the High Dive

I watched Big Phipps climb the high dive like he had nothing to lose. He looked dead-eyed, unbothered. The board drooped like a bottom lip.

"*BEANS*," one of his teammates yelled from below. The kid next to him in the ballcap cackled. It was an un-sanctioned nickname writ large, for which I was indirectly responsible. I wish I'd told them to can it, but reputation is a brittle thing.

Phipps' calf muscles tensed, the board groaned. But then he had second thoughts, made an about-face, shuffled toward the center of the board to collect himself.

Big Phipps.

Phippsy.

Slab of a kid.

A kid who, back in eighth grade, was recruited for varsity O-line despite the fact that he played more *Warcraft* than football. Special arrangements were made.

We sat next to each other in homeroom because our last names were neighbors. Made small talk, shared a love of Adam Sandler. Once he told me in confidence that he liked to hit the Taco Bell drive-thru, circle around and finish his burrito in time to order again at the intercom. He wasn't proud about it, but it was a game he knew he could win. I wish he'd never told me.

Phipps turned again on the board, made his way back to the edge. By now I couldn't see his eyes, but I'd have bet anything they were closed. Envisioning his teammates, who treated him more like a mascot than a comrade. Envisioning the faces of anyone who called him Beans. Who said, *C'mon, just pick me up.* Who said, *Phippsy'll finish what we don't.*

In Bio we'd been paired up to dissect a pig fetus. Phipps was surprisingly deft with the knife, made a clean cut from throat to anus like we'd been shown. He pointed out the spleen, let me take out the lungs.

"Kinda smells like a girl," he said of the formaldehyde.

I understood what he meant, but I didn't *know* what he meant. And I wouldn't until I was almost out of college. I had no reason not to believe him. We were a class of four hundred. Besides, he was kind. And he never asked how many people I'd told about his fast food solitaire.

After that, we shot finger guns at one another in the hallway. A few times he invited me over to finish lab work, play some Warcraft, but I always made excuses, stopped short of friendship. Convinced myself it was because we were a few months from graduation. My friends in Debate poked fun. *What's up with you and Beans?* Out of guilt I told them he hated that name, a burden they couldn't surmount.

It was five bucks to watch the contest. Most of the cash would go to Habitat, to the family whose house we seniors were going to build. Best belly flop of the day took home the rest, a hundred bucks to the restaurant of your choice.

Phipps had the burritos won before he even showed up. Everyone knew it; sucker's bets were made. All he had to do was jump, spread his limbs, let gravity do the rest. Give the people what they paid for. Emerge from the water pink and stinging, the victor. His closest competition was Ben Goff, who made up for a lower BMI with a high-voltage blend of commitment and lack of fear; his splash didn't even reach the lip of the pool.

There he is, Phippsy, I can still see him, the deft bounce that belied his bulk, the fold of his thighs, launching himself off the board, a refrigerator of flesh in a perfect parabola. And I wish I could say he pierced the water without a splash, a flawless incision that would have been a middle finger to us all. But I couldn't bring myself to look. No. I closed my eyes to the shattering water, to the collective groan, and understood he had played his role, given us a show.

Afterwards, I caught him in the parking lot, folding himself into his VW Rabbit, securing the gift card in the glove compartment. His hair was still spiky and wet. I leaned in through the passenger window, could feel my friends rolling their eyes behind me.

"Did it hurt, Phippsy?" I said. I suppose I wanted him to hit me with a finger gun, to tell me he'd hardly felt a thing.

What he said instead, as he shrugged, as his big mitt shifted the stick into first, was, "You tell me."

Hang Time

Nichols brought the ball up the court with controlled urgency. With twenty-three seconds left and his Roadrunners down one, it was go-time, but not panic-time. In moments like this—*in the clutch*—the game slowed down for Nichols. His teammates made their cuts like marbles through syrup. Every tick of the clock was an ocean of potential; every dribble a bookmark in space. This was *his* time. Like Coach Dunlow often told him in the quieter moments— after practice, or in the locker room before games; in any event out of earshot of his teammates—*You're our point guard, aright? Our floor general. Where YOU go, this TEAM goes.* So if nothing else, he owed it to the team to stay cool as a lizard in the shade. Central Valley District Championships didn't just happen after all, not to mention Aurelia Jackson— hair pulled back in a whip of a ponytail, glitter bomb on her cheeks—was right there in the bleachers: fourth stanchion, fourth row. And he had spotted one of the assistant coaches from The U—where he'd signed a letter of intent to go play ball next fall— wedged way up in the corner, where all coaches and scouts seemed to sit, as though they were private investigators or spies.

He pushed the ball past half court and with about twenty seconds to go, made eye contact with Witherspoon on the wing. Witherspoon was six-two or six-three, all sneakers and elbows, but he could shoot the leather off the ball from just about anywhere on the floor. Problem was, he was slow as a slug and couldn't jump over a credit card. Nichols knew he'd get some Division III offers, but turn them down and go to a state school to party and study Marketing or something. He waved Witherspoon off and his teammate quickly—gratefully—obliged, circling around beneath the basket to the opposite corner of the floor.

Seventeen seconds.

Nichols took a few dribbles to his right to fill the space Witherspoon had just left. Behind him, he heard Coach Dunlow—his voice as sandpapered as a battle-sieged general—holler, *C'mon now!*, one of those phrases that meant absolutely nothing, but which seemed to work nonetheless. The kid defending Nichols must have heard it too, because he grinned a little, revealing a mouthguard that was red and slick with spit, settled deeper into his defensive crouch and clapped his hands in a way that struck Nichols as both ironic and pitiable.

Fourteen seconds.

Freed from a screen on the low block near the basket, Ahearn, the Roadrunners' center, cut to Nichols' side of the court and kept his defender on his hip. He waved at Nichols wide-eyed with the universal sign for *Holy shit, I'm open*. Ahearn was a stud offensive lineman fielding several Division I offers, and really only played basketball because he got a kick out of manhandling other centers who weighed less than he did, which was all of them. Nichols respected Ahearn because he wasn't afraid of shit; he'd take the last shot without blinking. But he had about as much finesse as a jackhammer, and if, God forbid, he was fouled and sent to the free throw line? Well, they might as well pack it in and head home for *Jeopardy*. Nichols gave Ahearn a nod of the chin. Ahearn rolled his eyes and slapped his thigh in a show of frustration, then curled away to the other side of the lane. Now nothing stood between Nichols and the basket except for Mr. Mouthguard, and he wasn't at all worried about that.

Nine seconds.

Mouthguard licked his lips, sneered and clapped again. Not once did Nichols break eye contact. No. He stared right into Mouthguard's eyes and saw there a kid who wore gruff self-confidence as a cloak. Perhaps he had an older brother who used to kick his ass. Or perhaps he was from a well-to-do family and projected a disdainful arrogance to distract from his butter-soft upbringing. Whatever the case, he must have felt exposed, because he broke Nichols' gaze to glance over his shoulder to see if he had any defensive help. Big mistake. By the time he looked back, Nichols had already made his move, a right-to-left shimmying crossover dribble, to knife into the lane. Mouthguard pressed his body into Nichols' right side as he did his best to keep up. But it was too late: Nichols gathered the ball in two hands and planted his left foot for lift-off. He felt bodies closing in to his left so he double-clutched and swept the ball to his right hand for a low scoop shot with enough English that it would spin off the glass and into the cup.

Except he must have mis-timed his jump, because the ball rolled off his fingertips, took its low trajectory toward the basket and lodged fast into the crook of space between rim and backboard. Nichols' momentum carried him to the floor where he slid on his hip. He scrambled to his feet and fired a glance at the game clock—a shade under two seconds—then up at the ball where it held fast. He waited for the final buzzer to sound.

No sound came.

He looked back at the clock: it hadn't budged. The scorer's table must have stopped the clock for the dead ball, which meant the game . . . wasn't over?

The game wasn't over! Okay sure, possession would go to the other team and the odds were incredibly low—damn near impossible, really—but the Roadrunners could quickly foul and who knows, miracles can happen if you just believe.

Nichols looked to the scorer's table to confirm, but no one at the table was moving.

At all.

Not the terse grandma working the scorebook who now glared, unblinking, over the rims of her glasses in the direction of the basket as though it had insulted her personally. Nor the dad in the ballcap manning the clock who stared at the controller, mouth agape, like it had just pulled a quarter from behind his ear. Neither was Coach Dunlow, who stood stock-still with his face red and his hands clasped on top of his head in anticipatory anguish. And neither was the Roadrunners' bench where the assistant coaches and Nichols' teammates were all, every last one of them, stuck in contorted poses of agony and hope. Beyond the bench, the several hundred people in the stands were a mosaic of arrested motion: flailing arms and derpy faces and sparkly pom-poms and even a mini-explosion of Cheetos.

Now hold on . . . now just hold the *fuck on.*

Nichols spun and saw Mouthguard hanging in midair where he had collided with a fellow defender. His head was turned away to avoid his teammate's elbow and his eyes were scrunched tight and his lips were parted in a wince that revealed the flash of red rubber that protected his teeth.

He was stuck.

In midair.

Whatthefuck!

Nichols shot a look at Ahearn.

Frozen.

A rumbling mound of gleeful chaos caught motionless mid-stride on his way to gather Nichols' rebound.

He scanned for Witherspoon in the far corner: frozen, and flinching and generally shrinking from the moment.

Ohgodohgodohgod . . . what had he *done.* Sure, time had always seemed to shift into a lower gear for him in pivotal moments—what he attributed to his court vision and finesse—but this? No, this was very different. He cleared his throat and said— whispered, really—*Hello?* Then he said it louder— *HELLO*—and his voiced boomed around the concrete walls of the gym.

It was dead-silent, save for the low-grade industrial hum from the ductwork above, and Nichols' own breath, labored and heavy from his attack of the basket.

He went over to Ahearn and whispered his teammate's name: *Ahearn? Yo Ahearn! What the fuck you doing, man? Stop playing.*

He poked his teammate in the ribs. The mesh jersey fabric gave way and he felt the soft flesh beneath. But Ahearn didn't feel it. Or if he felt it, his thoughts and reactions were bottled up in that thick head of his.

Instinct and fear carried Nichols over to one of the referees, the one camped out at the baseline beneath the hoop. He was a thin man with thin, greying hair and his watery eyes were locked on the basket. His mouth was open a little and his whistle, on a string, had fallen from his lips and now dangled at his chest. Nichols waved a hand in front of the ref's face. Nothing. Then, for reasons he couldn't quite explain, he put the whistle back into the ref's mouth, pressed the lips together—grimacing as he felt the weird, prickly old man whiskers—to keep it secure. He hoped, stupidly, that the ref would blow the whistle and something, *anything*, would happen. But the ref didn't blow the whistle. He just stood there like a fucked-up Foot Locker mannequin.

THINK, Nichols. Thinkthinkthinkthink. Maybe he could restart the clock himself? Or like, call 911? And say what, exactly? That he'd managed to disrupt the space-time continuum in a musty high school gym?

Nichols took a deep breath to gather himself. *Calm. Down.* Almost unconsciously, he bent down to adjust his socks, a routine he relied upon to gather himself and set his focus before free throws.

First the left.

Then the right.

Setting the socks so they sat just below his calf.

He righted himself and took in another breath, let it out slow.

There.

That was a little better.

And maybe it was the rush of blood to the head, but to his surprise, the panic receded a bit and a strange sensation washed over him, something he hadn't felt in a very long time: absolute, unfettered independence.

He was not, for once in his life, being relied upon, scrutinized or evaluated.

He was . . . for the moment . . . *free?*

He turned his attention to Aurelia Jackson, wedged halfway up the bleachers behind the Roadrunners' bench. She stood with her hands clasped together beneath her chin, her eyes wide and her lips pressed tightly together as though she'd frozen in the middle of making an elongated *mmm* sound.

She looked beautiful.

Nichols had tried and failed not to fall for her—they'd only really got to know each other in Mr. Brathwaite's bio lab this semester—because in September they were heading off to schools a dozen states away from each other. They hadn't really begun dating so much as hanging out more or less all the time. They ate lunch together, took free period together in the library and often took the bus to Aurelia's family's place after school to do homework, which usually resulted in them retreating to Aurelia's bedroom before her mother got home from work. They'd yet to go to his house because after Mom passed, it was just him and Dad and the place was often a mess of clutter and dishes and usually at least one lightbulb needed replacing. Besides, he wasn't ready to let Aurelia into his life like that. Not yet.

He climbed the bleacher steps to the fourth row and shimmied past the other motionless students. Nichols reached and touched her cheek and when he took his hand away, his thumb had little sparkling flecks of glitter on it. The sight of it made Nichols sad. Because he knew, deep down, that it wasn't going to work between them. Sure, the summer would be fun and maybe they'd grow even closer, until, the night before they were to leave for school, they'd have an emotional, all-night conversation about how they'd try to make it work. Do the long-distance thing. Talk every day and visit each other when they could. And there was winter break, and really, the semesters were only three or four months long apiece, hardly any time at all. But Nichols knew that it was impossible, what with him having practice every day and all the travel, and certainly Aurelia herself would be busy with her own life and maybe *she* would be the one who would want the freedom, *to go out and see new people and try new things.*

Shit, he said aloud, and startled himself. He glanced around to see if Aurelia or the other kids in the bleachers had heard him. But of course they hadn't.

SHIT, he yelled. Why was he even here? In this jersey, in this gym, with the ball in his hands at the end of the game expected to *do* something. Like, why *couldn't* he just rescind his commitment to The U, and take a semester off before applying to Aurelia's school? What was stopping him from taking that kind of risk? He felt a thrill up his neck just thinking about it and he almost shook Aurelia with excitement in order to tell her all about his new plan. But then his attention drifted to the top row of the bleachers where the assistant coach from The U sat hunched forward, knees on elbows, chin in palm, eyes closed as though he'd peacefully dozed off for just a quick nap, a rest of the eyes.

That was why.

Not the coach specifically. But everything he represented.

Before Mom passed, she'd made him promise to get his degree. It wasn't some long, drawn-out emotional conversation or anything. Because that's not who Mom was. She had looked up at him from the bed she lay in, pallid and woozy from the morphine, and with the pursed lips she bore for every lesson or instruction she'd ever given him, rasped: *If you don't finish your degree, I will personally come back down to earth and smack you into February.* It didn't matter how he got his degree. If, by some miracle he made the league, or played in Europe, or semi-pro, or even if he tore up his knee and didn't play a minute at The U: he would finish school. In four years, or ten years, he'd get that piece of paper. And Nichols knew that this—that orange ball of pebbled leather wedged in the hoop—was his best chance to do so. Because if he was being honest, he wouldn't get into Aurelia's school on grades alone. And even if he did, the loans would be crippling. He could, in theory, stay local, go to the community college and live at home to help Dad, but after that? The reality was that companies weren't exactly banging down the door to hire CVCC grads. No. This was his chance, and he'd be damned if he would go and fuck it up.

Nichols looked again at Aurelia and almost said *I love you* out loud. He caught himself just in case everyone could still hear even if they couldn't move. But he thought it, and thought about how maybe he'd even tell her someday.

Nichols shimmied his way out of the row and went down the bleacher steps to the court where he made his way to the center circle. He looked at the ball wedged up there in the rim. He could, he

supposed, manipulate the outcome of the game. He
could jump up, poke the ball from its resting place
such that it dropped through the basket. Maybe then
everything would unstick and he'd go home a hero.
Or maybe that was dishonest and everything would
remain stuck because of it. Maybe the best thing to
do would be to knock the ball down and let the game
play out. By the rules of the sport, there would be a
jump-ball, which in high school, deferred to the
possession arrow, and that belonged to their
opponent. Despite his hope to the contrary, all of this
pretty much spelled a loss for the Roadrunners and
no championship banner to accompany the one from
'73. But punching that ball loose meant setting the
rest of Nichols' life in motion. And he wasn't so sure
he was ready for that.

He turned and walked to the other end of the
court, pushed open the aluminum door that led to the
locker room. He went in, found his locker, opened it
and removed his jacket. He put it on and flipped up
the hood. He went back into the gym, crossed the
court where all nine players and two refs were still
stiff as dummies, and went through the lobby, framed
on either side by glass cases that served as shrines to
Roadrunner athletic glories of yore. He shouldered
through the double doors and went outside.

The central valley wind whipped and whistled
through the parking lot. It was a clear night,
temperature in the low teens, and Nichols could see

his breath. Steam came off his exposed legs. It felt very good.

Soon, Nichols would go back inside, jump up and punch the ball free. For now, he closed his eyes, braced himself against the wind and let the minutes pass with hardly a thought at all.

Beanball

Harlan came to feeling groggy, like he'd swallowed Benadryl and Scotch. He remembered taking ball one, high and outside, then squaring up for the second pitch. He'd wound his bat around a few times like a windmill, his little pre-pitch ritual to show he still, at thirty-four, meant business.

After that? Nada.

Now he lay on his back and blinked up into the sun where a ring of eight faces peered down at him, a medley of curiosity and distress.

"Told you he ain't dead," said Runk, their catcher. He wacked Porter in the ribs with the back of his hand.

"You good, H?" Porter said. Porter played short, and so considered himself something of a leader.

Harlan blinked again, licked his lips, tasted sweat and dirt.

"Shouldna been crowding the plate," said a voice outside their perimeter. A few of Harlan's teammates turned to look, including Runk, who started like he was going to charge the guy.

"Hey fuck you, you dump," he spat, red-faced. "You almost took off his melon." Porter shushed him and corralled him like Harlan, and Runk, knew he would.

Harlan didn't blame the other pitcher. Did he have a bad goatee and dress in a full uniform like a grown child? Sure. But had Harlan been crowding the plate? Absolutely. He always had, just like his father had taught him. *Shrinks the strike zone*, he'd said to Harlan one afternoon at the sandlot when he was nine. *In this game, you gotta stare down some scary shit if you want to survive.* He was terrified as the pitches whizzed by his chin, but he did what he was told. He got the sense that this was his father's way of proving his love and that by holding his ground, Harlan was earning it.

"Rocked you right in the ear flap," Nuñez was saying to him now. He'd crouched down closer to Harlan and was patting him on the chest. "Don't worry about that jagoff. Guy thinks he's Wild Thing or some shit."

Nuñez was Harlan's closest friend on the team. Left fielder, still fast as a jackrabbit. He'd even played Double-A ball in Akron, the closest any of them had come to the Show. At first, they'd bonded over a love of the speedsters—Rickey Henderson, Kenny Lofton—but gradually, lubricated by two-buck pitchers at Connolly's, they shared bits and pieces of their own lives: Nuñez calling up photos on his phone of his twin girls dressed in frilly pink everything, Harlan telling Nuñez that he and Jessie were thinking about having a kid of their own. "Just do it, H," Nuñez had said. "Think of it like a nasty curve. You're never really ready." What Harlan stopped short of saying was that they'd already been trying. And trying. And trying. That the issue wasn't with Jessie, of that much they were sure.

"Take your time, H," Porter said, and as soon as he said it, Harlan heard the opposing pitcher chirp again, this time encroaching on their huddle.

"This is starting to feel like a forfeit, fellas. We get the dub, three-to-one?"

"Give us a goddamn second, chief," Porter said. "You cleaned his clock. You're lucky his eyes are open."

"Guess I put too much mustard on it for him," the pitcher said, real snotty, and that's all it took for Runk to twist up his face, chuck his cap in the dirt and spin off after the guy shouting, "Thought I said can your fucking yap." Porter ran after him, yanking on the ratty shirt with Runk's name and number on

the back (McGlovin on the front), which Porter had
pressed up for everybody.

Almost one by one, Harlan's teammates
peeled off to join the fray: Connors, the overweight
third baseman who owned the landscaping business,
Moyer in centerfield who taught science at the high
school, batted ninth and was always just thrilled to be
there, and even Tully at first base, who was pushing
fifty, had been divorced three times and drove an S-
Class. That left Nuñez, who dipped his head as if in
exhaustion. "Shit," he said under his breath. He
looked at Harlan and said, "I should..."

Harlan gave a little nod, so Nuñez stood up
and turned to throw his weight into the scrum,
which was now seventeen strong, a dusty, amorphous
waltz that had migrated to short centerfield.

Harlan closed his eyes, breathed in and out
slow. The shouts, the smell of baking dirt. The sound
of a sickening wet crack and then the sight of his
Little League teammate, Griffin Pepper, a name
Harlan would never forget, rolling on the ground at
home plate, screaming murder as blood sprayed—
actually sprayed, like a ruptured hose—from between
the fingers that covered his face. The pitcher was
already crying, the parents already rushing from the
bleachers. In the end, what had shocked Harlan most,
more than Griffin's broken nose, for that's what it
was, more than his high-pitched screams and the
blood that mixed with the dirt to form a rusty clay,

was that they had resumed the game after Griffin was helped off the field. And Harlan was up next. The pitcher who had hit Griffin in the face was a wreck, so they called in a reliever, a string bean with glasses who shakily sailed a few warmup pitches over the catcher's head into the backstop. While the pitcher warmed up, Harlan's father pulled him aside and put an arm around him. "What did we learn last week?" he asked.

"Toe the box?" Harlan said.

"That's right," his father said, squeezing his shoulder. "They can smell it if you're afraid. Be a man."

Harlan never got the chance to ask his dad who *they* were, just as he never got the chance to say, "I'm not even ten." He never got the chance because within six months, his dad was dead, ravaged by the cancer that had spread from his prostate, that he didn't even know was there.

He pictured the look on Jessie's face when he got home and told her what had happened. That, in a way, he'd almost been waiting for it his entire life. And he would tell her that before they met, back when all he cared about were these ballgames and the beers that followed, he never imagined he could love someone this much.

Harlan opened his eyes and gingerly removed his helmet, let it roll off his head. He slowly raised himself until he sat upright with his legs splayed out in front of him. His left ear was ringing a little, but the wooziness had passed. He spat into the dirt and observed the brawl-that-would-never-be. It seemed to have died down, thinned out to satellite shoving matches of four and five. He could still hear Runk's voice above everyone else's, Runk, who would play this role for life. This was the last time Harlan would see most of these guys. It wasn't so much a decision as it was a reality that had risen up to meet him. Not Nuñez though. Nuñez he'd stay in touch with, maybe even invite he and the wife and the twins over for mixed grill. He knew his childhood dream of being a ballplayer, the dream his father had passed down like a sacred heirloom, was officially ending on this scorcher of a Sunday in Southwest Ohio. He would go home and tell Jessie as much, tell her he was ready for the truth. And he would, for the first time in his life, admit that he was scared, like he should have done on an afternoon some twenty-five years ago, as his father started his windup, and he leaned too close to the plate, bracing himself for the oncoming rush.

They Played Enya at the Monster Truck Rally

I'm not even kidding. In retrospect, it makes some kind of demented sense, but at the time, me and Kara broke our protracted silence and looked at one another.

"No way," she said to me, squinting in her seat, as though to hear the music better. We could hear it fine. The speakers in the arena were cranked to lawsuit levels.

"Way," I said.

We bought tickets to avoid breaking up, thought we could channel our rage by proxy, watching two hours of breathtaking destruction up close and personal. Maybe it was a way for us to see how ugly things could get if we let them accumulate.

It was a terrible idea from the jump. We got a late start leaving the apartment—we fought about which doggy bowl to leave out for Winnie—and missed the first bash up. Gridlock traffic meant we had to park in the spillover lot, which was a mile away on foot. Kara hugged herself against a grey February wind and didn't look at me.

"This was your idea!" I said, but my words were swallowed up by the whirling gusts that spilled off the lake.

We found our seats in the upper deck and pissed off our whole row for making them stand just as the Soul Crusher launched thirty feet in the air, backlit by a glittering bomb of pyrotechnics in the smoky atmosphere of the arena. The lime green truck crunched down atop a decimated Oldsmobile station wagon and flipped on its roof like a mammoth turtle. The wheels spun in vain.

"Fucking hipsters," a red-bearded man said as we shuffled past.

"Oh shut up, we're just as broke as you," Kara hissed, so I had to intervene.

"She doesn't mean it," I said. "I mean she does, but not about you."

We took our seats and waited for the next spectacle. The emcee growled over the mic about how you could get your very own selfie with Thunder Buck, a recent Hall of Damage inductee, by the entrance to section sixty-nine.

"NICE," the emcee cackled.

There was a dance crew. They skipped out of the tunnel onto the dirt floor wearing mechanic's jumpsuits. The lights dimmed as an AC/DC b-side erupted from the PA. The dancers, all five of them, ripped off their jumpsuits in unison to reveal sequined bikinis that shimmered under the roving beams of light.

"Mega," said the pre-teen boy next to me. His mother clamped her palms over his eyes and said, "Lord have mercy."

"Indeed," Kara said.

I sat there and wished we knew how to talk things through. Without taking offense, without shutting down. But we were both so stubborn and insecure that we felt the need to win no matter the cost. Kara telling me I'd inherited my mother's meek obsequiousness. Me telling Kara she had a limitless selfish streak that sucked the oxygen out of any room she entered. Both were true, but we'd never admit it to the other.

We'd been engaged nine months. Deep down, I think we both knew that was as far as it would go. When our friends pressed us for a date, we told them we were taking our time, enjoying the engagement. The truth was we were snapping at each other, if we were talking to each other at all.

What do you do when you've grown apart? When the shift has happened slowly, day by day, like continental drift? I bought the ring hoping it might jolt us back to the way we'd been. When lightness came easy. When we would joke about how Kara once farted loudly in the Food Lion and blamed it on the poor pricing clerk. About how I was allergic to tree nuts, but loved chocolate-covered almonds so much that I was willing to swallow glass and feel my face swell to twice its circumference. Those days seem like they happened to different people, like they never happened to begin with.

We sat there in the nosebleeds, tickets I had bought at Kara's insistence for sixteen bucks a pop and watched as the batshit machines revved and hurtled and flipped, smashed into rusty old vans and the carcasses of dead washing machines. I wondered if they did this in other countries, or if we as Americans had such a thirst for destruction that we brought our children and got them corndog drunk as metal crumpled and glass exploded and choreographed flamethrowers roared to a blitzkrieg soundtrack.

Which is why the Enya tune was such a mindfuck. Kara reached over and touched my hand when the first notes emerged like smoke. I thought it must have been a reflex, an accident, but she didn't take it away. "Boadicea," one of the most beautiful songs humans have ever laid to tape, a fact we both agreed on when it played at Barcade on our first date. You know it, even if you don't know it. The haunting hum, the dirge-like synth. It's the one the Fugees sampled for "Ready or Not." The first few notes sound like they were recorded in the bowls of a warship. Which I guess makes it strangely appropriate for the finale of the Backyard Bash VI.

The emcee introduced Clever Trevor who was behind the wheel of Rammunition, a hot pink cab sitting atop tires the size of our studio apartment. Enya crooned, as if in mourning, as if warning us that if we weren't careful, we'd never be able to repair what was broken. Kara squeezed my hand. Clever Trevor revved his engine. It sounded like Godzilla clearing his throat. Rammunition's wheels spun, kicking up a great wave of red dirt, and shot off toward the ramp. The emcee promised us not one, not two, but THREE backflips. I didn't see how this was possible. Death and dismemberment were all but guaranteed.

Clever Trevor just about proved me right.

The hulking truck hit the ramp at top speed and launched into the air, somersaulting nose over ass—once, twice, three times—but Trevor must have mistimed his jump, because he didn't quite get the ass all the way back around on the final rotation. Rammunition landed grill first with a sickening crunch then sprung forward, a hot pink cartwheel, metal debris and glittering guts spraying all over the place to a chorus of *Oohhhhhs* until the severity of the wreck dawned on us.

The arena went quiet. No Enya. No emcee. A squadron of medical personnel sprinted from the wings carrying fire extinguishers. The kid next to me was crying into his mother's bosom. Kara was rapt.

"C'mon you asshole, *live*," she said through her teeth.

And as though he heard her prayer, Clever Trevor managed to climb from the wreckage, pulling himself free and standing atop the side of his truck as smoke billowed from the undercarriage. He looked tiny. An insignificant assemblage of bones and blood zipped up in a silver fire suit. He raised his fists in a V above his head and the crowd exploded as though they'd just seen a magic trick that forestalled the apocalypse. In some ways, they had. Without consciously doing so, Kara and I had joined the teeming masses on our feet. Kara hooked her fingers to her lips and issued a piercing whistle.

"I didn't know you could do that," I said.

"There's a lot I can do you don't know about," Kara said. Then she took my face in her hands and brought me in for the kind of sensuous kiss I never thought I'd experience again.

"Gross," said the kid to my left.

"Miracles make people horny," his mother said, and I felt Kara's lips spread into a smile.

In the car ride home, we were quiet, either basking in exhilaration or afraid to disrupt the newfound spark. At a blinking yellow light, I deigned to break the silence.

"Does this mean—" I said, but Kara interrupted me.

"Don't do that," she said. "Just drive."

She clicked on the radio and I prayed it might be another one of our songs. "This Must Be the Place." "Age of Consent." Hell, maybe even Enya again. Instead it was goddamn "White Wedding." It felt like a curse.

"Oh my god, yes," Kara said, and cranked the dial until I could barely hear myself think. She began to headbang in the seat next to me, her mop of black hair swirling about her face. Then she put her hand atop mine on the gearshift and flashed me a smile as I drove through the dark quiet streets that I knew so well, that I wished would unspool without end.

Rickey Henderson Sits by a Lake

May 1, '91. A's. Yanks. Bottom of the fourth. Rickey Henderson steals third, swipes Lou Brock's record from the books, yanks the bag out of the dirt and holds it aloft like sacrament, the Bay grey sky glinting off his wraparound shades. He clutches a mic, and with his mother, Brock himself and forty thousand in green and gold bearing witness, is swept up in the moment, issues eight words that will chase him forever: *Today, I am the greatest of all time.*

Everyone knows this part.

What if we don't know the rest?

What if, after the game, Rickey Henderson doesn't go home. Doesn't kiss his wife goodnight or tuck his three little daughters into bed. Steers a forest green Eddie Bauer past his glittering condo with regret searing his lips. Keeps the radio off because his thoughts are loud. What if he already knows they'll twist his words? *The greatest of all time? Where does he get off?* Make him sound cocky. Arrogant. Crazy. Shit, they already poke fun at him for referring to himself in the third person. What if he's always done this to admonish himself, because he cares so much? *Rickey, what the hell you doing chasing a two-one slider?* What if they simply asked?

What if Rickey Henderson steers his truck south on the 580, cuts east to Chabot Park in the purple twilight. Kills the engine and takes a deep breath, unclips his seatbelt. Gets out and walks toward the lip of the lake, hears the cicadas sing, a sound not unlike high heat whizzing past his ear. What if in the distance there's a golf course where he sometimes plays, even though he hates the sport, because when everything in your life is fast, you have to force yourself into a lower gear. What if he finds a bench and sits down, listens to the lake lap the shore, a liquid metronome. Counts the precious seconds in his head. Two-point-nine: the time it takes for him to steal second with a good jump. Three-point-one: the average pitcher-catcher throw out attempt. What if he told them about this? What if he told them about the stopwatch in his locker, the graph paper with the pencil scratch. The hours of game film, breaking down windups. Would it make a difference? Change the narrative? Would he find himself sitting on a bench by a lake in the fading light, mouthing the words, feeling their familiar shape? *Today, I am the greatest of all time.* What if he's been saying these words every day for as long as he can remember? What if today there just happened to be a microphone? What if his mother—who gave birth to him on Christmas day in the back of an Oldsmobile— once told him, *If you don't believe it, nobody will?*

What if they knew what Rickey knows? That they could say it too, that all it takes is a little courage.

What if, the night after he makes history, Rickey Henderson stands up from a park bench with a clear head, walks back to his truck, gets in and fires the engine. Merges back onto the freeway, lowers the windows, feels the cool spring air rush in. Begins to gain speed: seventy, eighty, ninety. What if the speedometer nips three digits, not because he feels free, but because he's already leaving those eight words behind. What if the what-ifs don't matter? What if this is just the beginning? What if a smile begins to take shape on Rickey Henderson's lips as he realizes something that will have the rest of the league chasing his shadow: if the words can't catch him, nothing can.

There's No Such Thing as a Lil Life

Lil Penny stands in line at Java the Hut waiting to order a thimbleful of espresso. He feels a tap on his shoulder, turns around. It's a guy in his early thirties peering down at him wearing a snapback Suns cap and a look of polite contrition. Lil Penny knows what's coming.

"Hey bro, hate to bug you," the guy says. It's what they always say. What Lil Penny never says is, *Yeah so why did you?*

"Huge fan is all. Grew up on those Nike ads. Had the kicks and everything."

Lil Penny nods along. The guy looks as though he wants to be congratulated. Or told his childhood was worth something.

"Thank you, brother," Lil Penny says. "I appreciate it."

Now the guy looks surprised. Because Lil Penny isn't the cocky blowhard he played on television with Anfernee and Tyra. He's gracious, understated. Keeps to himself. When he first settled in Tucson, these incidents happened more frequently. Now folks around town know to let him be. They know he moved out here for the quiet life. Took that Nike money and bought a small ranch where the saguaros are five times his height. Runs the community puppet theater in the strip mall between the European Wax Center and the H&R Block. Turned down a line of toys and a movie franchise out of respect for his namesake. Because when Anfernee tore up his knee, Lil Penny saw a version of himself out there writhing on the parquet, a dream cruelly snatched away. So he made it his mission to give back, nurture the dreams of the marionettes in his troupe.

"You think it would be possible," the young man is saying, but Lil Penny is already shaking his head. This time he's the one who's contrite. But he stands firm. No autographs. Partly because it's a bitch for him to hold a Sharpie in his tiny hand, but mostly because he knows they often wind up on eBay, a cynical money grab.

The young man looks crestfallen, so Lil Penny tells him, "But I appreciate the love, my man," and turns around, shuffles forward in line to order.

"The usual?" the barista says to him with a warm smile. She has to crane over the edge of the counter to see him.

Lil Penny nods. "And whatever the young man behind me is having," he says.

In moments like this it's hard not to imagine what might have been: sitting in the director's chair, on stage clutching a gold statuette. But he shakes away the daydream, knows the work he's doing is important enough. After his coffee, he will make his way over to the theater, help his students prepare for this weekend's performance of *Guys and Dolls*. And he'll remind them of something his mother told him every morning as a kid getting ready for school: The world will try to convince you otherwise, but Baby, you're nobody's puppet.

The Reign Man Parts the Clouds

When the clouds descend in a gummy fog, a deep grey funk that seeps from my pores, keeps the curtains drawn and the pantries lean, I lie in bed and submit to the screen. Mixtape prescription. Number forty in serotonin green and gold attacking the rim again and again and again. A buoyant crush of ferocious joy to remind us such an approach to life is even possible. Coast-to-coast tomahawks. Reverse double-pumps. Put-backs, baby-cradles, the soaring oop to Gary Payton's alley. Each punctuated with some version of the artist's signature: a roar or a shimmy or a crouch and a point and a stare down, none of it mean-spirited, all of it saying, *Shit, I didn't see it coming either.* And the haze parts for a moment or two because to see the Reign Man bring the thunder down on someone else's head, to see the posterized body beneath the hoop in a crumpled heap of regret and shame, is to know that we do not suffer alone.

Tully

I am your archetype, a lurker of tunnels. Hands
taped, I pace the dripping furnace. Somewhere above,
the announcer growls my name. On the lips of
strangers, it's a synonym for wicked, the relentless
enmity on which I depend. Ferocious, they say.
Caged beast. Can barely spell his own name. Maybe
it's true. Maybe I am what they want me to be.
Maybe I am my country's son.

      I was a weightless child, a chaser of bricks.
They plucked me from rubble, welded my hands.
They fed me fire; their champagne dreams became
my own. Someday soon I will forget my mother's
face.

      A whisper, paper-thin, tells me it's time.

      I prowl the maze, bow in a bowl of smoke.
Thousands of faces, brutal as pastries, scream of
forfeited wars. They gamble on flesh, can taste the

collision. Flashes pop, the wicked lithium. A man with a haggard visage grips my wrists; I touch the fists of a stranger. He looks just like me: tattooed conscience, kaleidoscope eyelids. Terrified.

Tomorrow, ink will spill, pens fueled by his blood. In an hour, lying in a bed of regret, he will forsake his trade. In minutes, the pitiless nexus; the fantastic damage. He will crumple at my feet, a heap of bones, a natal shape.

He believes the same will become of me.

For now, my corner is babel, a lash of tongues. I loom, a brooding razor. I coil for the knell, the stinging bell.

I hope it never comes.

Wishbones

I was the main event, the man you paid to see. I was oblivion, a crush of air, a brutal punch. In the open field I was fast as silk. You didn't know you didn't have me until I was already gone.

I made teammates throw knuckles on more than one occasion. Fans would laugh: *Fools decked each other in the headgear.* But we players understand. You smash your fist into someone's helmet because deep down you want to hurt yourself, not the other man behind the midnight mask. Damage is less scary if you cut out the middleman.

The moment it all ended didn't happen in slow motion like everyone says. That's just a way to give it meaning. But there is no meaning. There is before. And there is after.

Before: third and six, man in motion, sixty thousand breathing fire. The ball is snapped like a starting gun and shoved into my gut and I am a cannonball seeking casualties and the vast openness beyond.

After: I am on the ground. I try to stand, but I topple over because my left leg barely exists. I look around and my teammates are covering their eyes and the opposing safety is on all fours with orange leaking out his facemask and our center, a slab of a man, is blubbering, saying, "Ohgodohgodohgod" like it's something to believe in. It's when I look at my leg that I realize the resonant sound of a wishbone crack wasn't the pop of a tackle but an emotionless law of physics. I black out just as the trainer drapes a towel over my leg like a corpse.

Now I sit for interviews and they ask me would I do it all again. The punishment. The violence. The smug look on their faces knows I will say no. That I would take it all back. Avoid the cane. Avoid the pain. That I will never let my boy play.

But I say, Yes. Of course I would do it again.

Your career ended in a nightmare, they say.

A nightmare is coming for all of us, I say. Doesn't matter if it's at the end of your career or at the end of your life or somewhere in between. But not many can say theirs came at the end of a dream come true.

My boy has the dream. Came up with it all on his own. I see the way he moves, his piston legs, lightning feet. He has my blood and the hunger to match. Someday his dream will come true. He will run the only way he knows how. Just watch.

An Empty Ballfield is a Pocket of Peace

I wake up in a heap of blankets on Mom's bedroom floor. My brain flashes and I sit up to make sure Mom didn't get sick while I was asleep, but she's not even in her bed and the trash can isn't there anymore and I hear pots and pans in the kitchen.

Wish somebody would tell me what I'm supposed to do. To sit down next to me and say, Dustin, don't worry, I'll take it from here. Or, Dustin, all you need to do is tell your mom how much you love her, and she'll take care of the rest, just you see. But I can't think of who that somebody would be, so I get up and carry my blankets and pillow to my room and dump them on my bed and get dressed for practice, leaving behind the batting glove she gave me so I don't have to think about her on the field.

In the kitchen, Mom is blowing smoke from a cigarette out the window over the sink. Her breath makes the Minnie Mouse ornament that hangs from the window dance and spin.

"I know, Dustin," she says, feeling me there. Her voice sounds like she ate sandpaper. "You don't have to say a word."

But I do say a word. I have to. Because maybe if I'm honest, something will click into place. Maybe she'll try to be better.

"I was worried," I say. "I slept on the floor all night." I go to the cabinet and get the Mini Wheats and get the milk and pour myself a bowl.

"How long did Chuckie stay?" Mom says.

"He didn't," I say.

Mom nods, sucks down the last of her cigarette, taps it out in the ashtray on the counter with a shaky hand. I sit at the table and watch her pour herself some rum.

"Hair of the dog," she says. "Someday you'll need it too."

"Don't you have work?" I say, my voice shaky.

"Called in," Mom says. "You want me to drive you?"

I shake my head. "I'm meeting up at Jasper's," I say, even though I'm not.

Mom nods again, runs a hand through her short hair. "I know I'm a bad mother," she says and looks at me to see what I'm going to say.

I finish the last of the soggy Mini Wheats, suck the sugar off my tongue, then tip back the bowl and drink down the milk to keep from crying. I get up and put the bowl carefully in the sink and say, "I still love you," and Mom's shoulders start to shake, because that's the meanest thing I could ever think to say.

Not sure how many miles it is to the practice field, but it takes me an hour to get there and by the time I do, I'm sweating through my shirt. I'm the first one and practice still doesn't start for another half hour.

The field is empty and quiet. No shouting. No clapping. No ping of the bat or the smack of the ball hitting the mitt. And for now at least, no Zacky. Just the zipper sound of bugs and the swoosh of the breeze through the leaves. I sit on the metal bench by first base and hold my mitt up to my face and smell it and the smell of the leather and dirt and sweat calms me down. When Dad took me to get my first mitt at Walmart, the same one where Mom works now, we rode over in his truck and listened to the Townes Van Zandt tape, his favorite. We didn't talk too much, like usual. Something I liked about Dad was that he only asked questions if he really wanted to know the answer, not just because he wanted to fill the space or because he thought he was supposed to ask questions about my life. This was also when he and Mom were starting to fight more, so maybe his brain was full of arguments that hadn't started yet and there was no room for questions, even if he wanted to ask them. We went to the aisle with all the tennis rackets and basketballs and baseball mitts and Dad just said, "Pick one." I tried not to get too excited because Dad was always so even when he wasn't fighting with Mom, but I could barely keep it in. Plus, the only other time I was allowed to pick something out was after Dad showed me *Call of the Wild* and I told him I loved it, he brought me to Waldenbooks at the mall and said I could choose a book because reading books makes you a more well-rounded person. I picked a *Goosebumps* one called *The Haunted Mask* because everyone at school was talking about it and I liked the cover and Dad read the back and said, "You gonna have nightmares?" I shook my head very serious, and he laughed and said, "Course not," and I never told him that I read the book in one day and couldn't sleep for a week. At Walmart, I think I tried out every single glove on the rack, not just to make sure I got the right one, but so I could make the moment last longer. I knew which one I wanted all along—the black Rawlings with the Ken Griffey Jr. signature in gold in the palm—but I pretended like it was the hardest decision of my life. Dad laughed and said, "It ain't a wife. You'll outgrow the sucker in a couple years anyway." Then he blinked and said, "Hell, maybe it is like a wife." And I finally held up the black Rawlings mitt that felt soft and snug on my hand, and Dad said, "That the one?" and I nodded, and he checked the tag and snorted and said, "How'd I guess?" and I held my breath, but he said, "Let's roll."

Back in my room that afternoon, I stretched rubber bands around the web of my new mitt and put it under my mattress to break it in and sat on my mattress and listened to Mom and Dad talk and then talk louder and then fight, until Dad knocked on my door and came in and said, "Sorry pal, I'm gonna need it back," and I didn't even cry or complain, because Dad looked so tired, and I got up and took the mitt out from my mattress and took the rubber bands off and gave it back to him and he took it and went back to Walmart and came back with a brown one that was stiff as plastic, but I pretended to love it and Dad pretended like he didn't know I was pretending. The glove I have now is

Coach Dunlap's from when he was a kid because last season, he saw how beat up my old one was and that it barely fit anymore and he showed up to practice one day and called me to his car and just said, "Trade you, boss," and we never talked about it again.

Just to see what it feels like for once, I jog around the bases slow, like David Justice did the other night against the Rockies, like the ball I crushed is still looking for a place to land, and as I circle third and head for home, Coach Dunlap's red Cherokee turns into the lot and I hear the bass and drums of his stereo even though the windows are closed and he cuts it off right as I stomp on home plate.

He gets out of the car and smiles and says, "Game winner?" so I say, "Bottom of the eleventh," and he says, "Rad."

I go over to his truck and help him unload the bucket of balls and the bases and the netted bag of clacking helmets.

"Been here a while?" he says.

"I thought we started at eleven today."

Coach Dunlap looks at me and I know he doesn't believe me because we've had practice at noon going back to last season.

"I don't want to get all in your biz or nothing, but, you good?"

I hoist the bag of helmets onto my shoulder to keep myself from crying and I'm confused, because it's not that I'm not good, it's that where would I even start if I wanted to explain?

Coach Baker's Tahoe pulls up, so I wouldn't be able to explain anything right now anyway, and Coach Baker and Derek get out of his car, and Coach Baker

looks at us and says, "Look at these two bruisers," and
Coach Dunlap says, "Hidey ho," and then looks back at
me and lowers his voice and says, "Just think of me like
a big bro or something. But only if you need."

I nod and bite my cheek hard and wish I could
hug him, but instead I tap his fist with mine.

Me and Derek throw to each other to warm up
in the outfield while we wait for the rest of the guys to
show up. Derek looks relaxed. He's got sunglasses on
that wrap around his face and that bend the light pink
and gold and blue. He's chomping gum, now and then
blowing a bubble that he sucks in with a click. I study
him for things I don't have, and it feels like everything:
the wristbands, the shining glove, the confidence. The
lack of fear that doesn't come from strength, no, but
from not even knowing all there is to be scared about.

Derek points his glove to my right, so I start to
run to my right, and he throws a lob way out there, so I
sprint to catch up to it and stick out my glove and nab it
right in the web.

"Nice one," he says and claps the side of his
mitt, and he means it.

I point my glove to the left, so Derek takes off
running and I toss him a lob and he catches up to it
easy. He tosses the ball back to me and says, "C'mon
Dust, put some juice on it," so this time I don't even
point my glove, I wind up and throw a low arching line
drive to his left and Derek goes, "Ah," and takes off
running, then harder still, then lays out with his left arm
stretched way out and the ball bounces in the grass, just
out of reach. He gets up laughing and says, "Almost
had it," and I realize I don't really hate him. It's that I

wonder what I would be like if I *were* him, the kind of person whose brain isn't a messed-up radio. I wonder if he knows that Katie Wright likes him instead of me, or that that's the rumor, or that that's what Dylan thinks the rumor is. Except it doesn't matter because Katie saw Mom being a rum zombie at the Campbell Park fireworks and she saw Chuckie being a cop and she saw me being scared, and so of course she likes the guy with confidence and no radio in his brain.

"Again," Derek is saying, so I wind up and toss the ball in the exact same spot, except this time Derek is ready. He takes off like a sprinter at the gun and his arms are pumping and his legs are pistons, and he dives outstretched and the ball lands right in the pocket of his shiny black mitt like there's nowhere in the universe it would rather be.

We work on bunts during practice, which look so easy on TV, but which are really hard and scary too, because all you have is a thin stick of metal protecting your neck, chest and face from the heat-seeking ball.

"Remember," Coach Baker says, squatting at the plate with a bat in front of him like a shield, "We want soft hands. Bunts are all about touch, right?" He sticks the bat out with stiff arms like a robot and says, "We're not here," then he bends his elbows and brings the bat in tighter and moves it around a little like he might start to dance with it. "We're here. Soft and smooth."

Shelsky and Jasper both put bunts right down the first baseline and sprint to first kicking up dust and they make it because they're the fastest. Derek gets up and bunts a popup right back to his dad and then chucks his helmet in the dirt, so his dad hollers, "HEY. The hell you doing? Three laps," so Derek takes off running around the diamond. Duckworth bunts one hard to third and chugs to first and gets thrown out easy and then Alvarez gets on base, and he laughs and claps and then it's my ups.

I dig in close to the plate like always and as Coach Baker winds up, I square to bunt and my heart thuds and I flinch and the ball hits the end of my bat and the bat buzzes and vibrates and my hands go numb, but there's no time because I'm sprinting to first and the world is bouncing and Derek is yelling at Duckworth behind the plate and by the time I get to first, the ball is still sitting right on the edge of the baseline about halfway to first and Duckworth and Derek are arguing about who's ball it was and Coach Baker is saying, "Y'all gotta communicate," and Coach Dunlap is clapping and smiling wide and spits a jet of brown juice into the dirt and yelling, "Way to BE, Dusty baby, way to BE. You all take notes on Dusty, THAT is how you hustle, like a turd after coffee." And I can't help but smile even though he might just be saying that because he thinks he has to.

After practice, we gather around and Coach Baker tells us about Granite Planet, who he thinks we can beat and that we're due for a win because we don't practice hard and work our keisters off to lose three in a row and how about it? And we all clap super determined like beating Granite Planet is the only thing that matters in life." OnetwothreeTEAM," we say in the huddle, and then I turn to Dylan and say, "Hey," and he says, "Hey," and I slap Jasper on the shoulder with the back of my hand and as we go back to the bench to wait for our rides, I ask them if they want to hang out all of us together.

Dylan smiles and says, "Okay, yeah when do you guys want to come over?" so I shrug and say, "Whenever," and Jasper says, "You really got a BB gun?"

"I showed Dustin how to shoot," Dylan says.

"Did he suck?" Jasper says.

"At first," Dylan says and laughs, "But then he started to suck less," and that's all I can ask for in life, really, to suck less and less as I go.

"Let's hang out at my house," Jasper says, because he's afraid of seeing Dylan's mom in her wheelchair dying of Lou Gehrig's disease, but I bite my tongue. "You guys can sleep over. We can shoot BBs in the woods behind my house, and I can kick your asses in *Mortal Kombat*."

"I'll bring *Pet Sematary*," Dylan says. "Or maybe *It*. Or both and we can pick. Or we can stay up and watch both."

"What are you bringing?" Jasper says meaning me, and I have nothing to bring, except maybe Dad's old pack of cigs.

"I'll find something," I say.

We watch a boxy yellow Volvo pull into the lot and Dylan says, "That's my cousin," and he gets up off the bench. He holds out a palm, so I slap it. He holds out a palm to Jasper and Jasper slaps it, but from the bottom up, so if Dylan was holding out popcorn to share it would fly out of his hand and scatter in the dirt. Dylan makes a fist and jukes like he's about to punch Jasper in the chin with an uppercut, and this makes both me and Jasper flinch, and Dylan laughs and says,

"What are you so afraid of?" Then he says, "Later," and goes to get into his cousin's car and waves from the passenger seat as his cousin drives out of the lot.

"See?" I say.

"See what?" Jasper says.

"Told you he's cool."

"Maybe. No way I was going to his house. It's probably cursed."

"Maybe," I say, but I think he's probably right and that I'm probably cursed too since I went there last week to hang out and especially since I stole money from his mom's purse.

Jasper's Mom pulls up in the station wagon so we both get up and take our gloves and Jasper takes his bright blue bat and we make our way to the car and as we do, Jasper stops short and says, "Oh shit," so I say, "What?" and before he can answer, I see too.

At the end of a row of parking spaces, near the trees, standing up and looking at us over the open driver's side door of an all-blue Chevy Blazer is Dad.

I KNEW IT!

Knewitknewitknewitknewitknewitknewitknewit.

My legs want to run toward him and away from him at the same time, so they don't move at all.

"Did you know he was coming?" Jasper says, and his mom honks the horn in her station wagon like, "Hello?" because she doesn't know why we stopped.

My brain is all static and foggy and it's hard to take deep breaths and I feel like I might pass out.

"You going to go over?" Jasper says, but I'm already drifting toward my dad, away from Jasper, away from his voice saying, "Okay, later," and my cleats are chewing the gravel in the lot and Coach

Dunlap is parked a few spaces over and loading the gear into his red Cherokee and he sees me walking toward the Blazer and looks at Dad and looks at me with a concerned look on his face.

Dad smiles through a beard that's longer than I've ever seen it and he taps his hand twice on the frame of the door. He steps around and shuts the truck door so there's nothing between us and he's wearing jeans and boots and a t-shirt that says EVERGLADES NATIONAL PARK on it, and he says, "Some bunt."

"What?" I say and it comes out like a whisper, like my voice doesn't actually believe it's talking to Dad for the first time in almost a year, like maybe he's really a ghost like Zacky.

"You good, Dust?" Coach Dunlap says from the driver's seat, through the open passenger window.

"He's just fine, thank you," Dad says.

I start to say, "This is my—" but Dad cuts me off and says, "I'm his father."

Coach Dunlap nods, but he doesn't look too convinced. "Ole Dusty is a fine ball player. Takes guts to step in the way he does. Specially at this age."

Dad smiles big and says, "Taught him that."

"Jamie Dunlap," Coach Dunlap says and raises two fingers.

"Alright now," Dad says.

Coach Dunlap nods and looks at me like, *You sure you're good?* and even though I don't know, I nod. "Alright then. See you boys," Coach says, then backs his Cherokee out of the lot and it's just me and Dad and the swelling whistle of the cicadas.

"How'd you know I had practice?" I say and it's not what I imagined saying to Dad when I pictured seeing him in my head, but then again, I'm more confused than I thought I'd be.

"What, no hug?" he says.

So I go in and hug Dad and he presses me up against his chest and he smells like sweat and smoke and burnt metal just like I remember.

"Damn, you're big," he says, pushing me away to get a better look. "How'd you get so big?" I shrug, so he says, "You happy to see me?" I nod, then the tears I was holding in from way before decide now's the time and I blink and they all come shooting out at once and Dad says, "Hell," and brings me in for another big hug.

"You hungry?" he says, and I nod because if I shook my head no, I'm afraid I'd never see him again. "C'mon."

We get into Dad's truck, and he starts it up with a rasp and a rumble and it smells like hot leather and too-sweet vanilla from the yellow tree swinging from the rearview mirror, and a voice on the radio is shouting about smoooooth ice cold French vanilla coffee from Dunkin.

Dad looks at me and smiles and his teeth are yellower than I can remember, and he takes a hand and wobbles my head around so my hat falls low over my eyes and he says, "Why'd you have to go and get so big for?"

"I didn't try to," I say, "It just happened."

"Tell me about it," Dad says.

We slide into a booth at Denny's and flip through the thick laminated menu and the hunger hits me like a punch and my stomach moans and gurgles so loud that Dad hears it and laughs.

"She feeding you?" he asks.

Hearing Dad refer to Mom means he still thinks about her, about me, about us.

"What are you getting?" I say.

Dad lets his breath whistle out his nose. "Now that's a good question."

He examines the menu, his brown eyes scanning the pages, his dark hair thinning above his forehead, the dirt under his nails. None of this feels real.

"I'ma go with an omelet. Sausage, peppers, cheddar, whole wheat toast and a Mr. Pibb." He shuts the menu like case closed and looks up and says, "I could eat breakfast all day, every day if they let me."

"Who's they?"

"Nobody," Dad says. "Life. You like breakfast?"

I nod.

"Course you do. You used to love those, what are they called—" He snaps his thick fingers to help him remember.

"Frosted Mini Wheats."

"Yessir," Dad says, then he waves down a waitress and says, "Miss, y'all got those Frosted Mini Wheats? My son here eats them by the silo."

The waitress is a big lady with curly red hair, a yellow collared shirt with a tag that says April. "The cereal?" she says. "I can check for y'all."

"That's okay," I say and both she and Dad look at me like they're surprised I know how to talk. "I want a burger medium-rare with Swiss cheese, tater tots and a side of bacon."

"Man knows what he wants," April says.

"Alrighty," Dad says, grinning, probably because she called me a man. He places his order and hands the waitress the two giant menus and she says, "Coming at you quicker than you think," and disappears behind a pair of swinging metal doors into the kitchen.

"Her name was April," I say, and what I mean is, Mom's name is only a few months after that, which really means, What happened to our family? which really means, I'll do anything to make you stay, to make you love us again.

"You been reading?" Dad says.

"Yeah," I say. "We got assigned *Watership Down*."

Dad nods like he approves. "Been a while for me. Hazel and them, right?"

"I like it so far. It's a lot of pages though."

"Stick with it. Little bit each day. Reading helps you understand people. I really believe that. My old man thought reading was for sissies. But I disagree. I say you can have a tough hide and appreciate a good story at the same time."

"I liked when you used to read to me before bed."

"I liked that too," Dad says. He reaches over and picks up the pepper shaker, turns it around in his hands. "Peaceful, wasn't it."

"I miss it."

This makes Dad look at the table and clear his throat. Then he looks up at me and leans back and puts an arm over the back of the booth like we're two old friends about to share some stories. "I know you're wondering why the hell I'm here. Honestly, I'm not even sure I know the answer to that. I left one place and found myself in another."

"Did you find it?" I say.

"The place?"

"No. Your true calling?"

Dad squints his eyes. "What's that, a riddle or something?"

"No, the book," I say. "The one in the attic. I found it up there."

Dad looks at me, but through me, then his face reforms itself and his eyes click back to reality. "Shoot, you found that?" He scratches the side of his beard, looks back over his shoulder like he wants to ask our waitress, Where's our food at, then looks back at me. "I don't say this about many books, but that one's all a bunch of bull. I just wish I'd learned that sooner instead of chasing my tail. Find something you're good at and do it. Don't get me wrong, books can teach you a lot about life. But dreams are what you wake up from when it's time to go to work. Best for a man to learn that early."

"What are you good at?" I say and Dad laughs with a flash of yellow teeth through his beard.

"That is the sixty-four-thousand-dollar question."

"I don't know the answer either."

Dad's smile fades away and he says, "Don't give me that. You wanna know what you're good at?"

I shrug.

He points a finger at my chest. "Having a big heart. I can see it. Everybody can see it. Just don't let this world break it because it will damn sure try."

"So what do I do with it?"

"Whatever it tells you to do."

And I start to wonder if it was my heart that told me to burn the photo of the naked lady from the *Penthouse* me and Jasper found in the woods and smash the gnome in my neighbor's yard and hate Chuckie for taking Dad's place and steal Silly String from the Shitty Kitty and money from Mom's purse and even more money from Dylan's mom's bedroom drawer, but then April comes to our booth and says, "Lunch is served, boys," and slides our plates in front of us. "Can I get y'all anything else?" she says, and Dad says, "A time machine if you can swing it," and she says, "Shoot if we had one of them, this place would have no staff," then she laughs to herself until she coughs and walks away.

I dump some ketchup on the cheese on my burger and another dump on my plate for the fries and pass the ketchup to Dad, who puts it on top of his omelet in a thick straight line and I eat a slice of bacon and another one quick because it's impossible not to.

"Slow your roll," Dad says. "It don't have legs."

We eat our food in quiet for a little while.

Then Dad says, "It wasn't your fault."

"I know," I say quick, even though it's been a thought in the back of my head like a pebble in my shoe.

"I mean it," Dad says. "I didn't want things to go the way they did. Neither did June. But when something real heavy happens, a wall can go up between two people that gets thicker and thicker until eventually you're both in separate rooms and there are no windows or doors anymore and you forget what the person on the other side of the wall is really like or why you ever loved them and you start thinking the same thing about yourself."

What am I supposed to say to that? I can't tell if Dad wants me to say, I forgive you, or Everything will be okay, or Let's all work together to break down the wall.

"Where did you go?" I say.

"Let's see now," Dad says and ticks off on his fingers: "Savannah, then Tampa, then Stetson and Orlando, then back up to Tampa, then voila."

"You were an electrician in all those places?"

"Sometimes. Sometimes not."

"What were the not times?"

Dad wipes his mouth with his napkin and says, "They fill you up with more questions the older you get?"

"I think so," I say.

"You go up in the attic?"

I nod.

"What you do up there?"

"What you taught me. Read. Think."

"You're your daddy's son I'll give you that."

"I see Zacky sometimes."

Dad coughs a little as he chews. "You what now?"

"He comes to visit me. He wears my old overalls, and I can't ever really tell when he's going to show up."

Now Dad looks scared like maybe he regrets picking me up. "Sometimes I see him in my dreams too, Dust," he says, like he hopes that's what I mean.

"Not in my dreams. Like, here. Like, in this booth maybe."

Dad chews the last of his omelet, then takes a long drink of Mr. Pibb. "It's good to have an imagination," he says. "Sometimes when I was alone on the road, I'd pretend I was Townes, up on a stool, singing songs to a small room, that—"

"It's not my imagination," I say, getting angry, so Dad puts his hands up, one of them a fist with his wadded-up napkin. "Okay," he says, "Alright. I believe you." Then: "What do y'all talk about?"

"He doesn't talk. But I can like, tell what he's thinking."

"I understand," Dad says, trying not to look worried. "Does June know?"

I shake my head. "She wouldn't get it."

Dad sucks his teeth and wipes a hand down his face, looks around for April.

"Y'all talk about him at all?" he says.

"Sometimes. We went to his grave for his birthday."

"Shit," Dad says and shakes his head. "I wish I could fix it all, Dust. Take away the pain. I would take it all if I could. More than I already have. June's too."

"Do you think you and Mom will ever get back together? Is that why you're here?"

"That what you want?"

The question is so direct that hearing it out loud makes me wonder if that is what I want, if maybe what I really want is just the calm before any of this started, calm in my brain and in my gut, calm before Zacky was even born and then died, before I ever knew his name. If what I want is just impossible.

"Maybe," I say. "If you don't fight anymore."

"I'd start with her not having me arrested."

"She says you're not holding up your end of the bargain."

"It's far from a bargain, son. She dating a cop?"

"How do you know?"

"People got big mouths," he says. "That much will never change."

***

Dad takes a pack of cigs from the glove compartment, taps one out, puts it to his lips, cups his hands around it and flicks a red lighter until the metal scrapes up a flame. He holds out the pack to me and I reach to take one.

"I was kidding," he says, yanking the pack back and blowing out smoke. "Twelve is way too young for heaters."

I don't correct him.

We take the long way home, out past the camel hump hills where the cows chomp and graze, past the gas station with the good corndogs, past a curve where a nest of twenty mailboxes fight for space like baby birds.

"Do me a favor," Dad says over the wind roaring in through his window, over Townes singing about some lady he'll never see again, "Don't tell June I'm back, aright? Not yet."

I look out the window, watch summer blur by and wonder if maybe there's a chance.

"What if I do?"

Dad bends the Blazer around the curve just as a Mac truck with no haul attached bombs past in the other direction, rocking our car like a Hot Wheels toy.

"I'd prefer to do this my way," Dad says.

"What's your way?"

"I haven't quite figured that out yet, but I think it involves doing something nice."

We dip over a hill and through a tunnel of trees that chops up the sun into bits, so it sprays over the car and over our faces and bodies through the windshield and I think about how we went to the zoo one time as a family, the Christmas lights glowing like a million stars and I get a little giddy.

"You know what I remember?" I say.

Dad either doesn't hear me or is waiting for me to finish.

"When we went to the zoo, all four of us. At Christmas time. Maybe we could all go again sometime."

Dad looks at me and smiles and for once I came up with a good idea. He reaches over and wobbles my head again, so I have to straighten my hat one more time and as I do, Dad says, "Hell, I wish I had your memory."

Dad pulls over to the curb a few houses down from ours and shifts into park but leaves the engine gurgling.

"Mom's not home," I say, "She took a second job."

"Not sure I'm ready to see the house," Dad says and tries to smile. "Is she still—" He sorta winces and runs a hand down his chin and pulls his beard like he's trying to wring water from it.

I know he means is she still drinking heavy like she was after Zacky died, in the way that built up the walls Dad was talking about, and part of me wants to say Yes, even more now too, and just yesterday, Chuckie had to carry her from Campbell Park and put her in his police car like she was a big doll, but the other part wants to protect Mom, to say, No, she is trying to do what's best, and she took another job because you aren't holding up your end of the bargain, and she has a new boyfriend because Moms deserve to be happy too, and maybe both things can be true, so what I say is:

"I need to feed Sauce."

"Who?" Dad says and cocks his head.

"My fish," I say. "I forgot to feed him this morning."

Dad half-laughs and nods his head, so I hold out my hand and Dad looks at it and half-laughs again and takes my hand, so I shake it and squeeze hard and Dad squeezes back, but not too hard, in a way that says: I love you and I love your mother and this might end in peace or it might end in chaos and I wish this world was fair, but this is the world we got, a world where I'm shaking your hand in a truck parked out of sight of the house I raised you in and I know this isn't enough, but maybe enough is coming for us soon, we'll just have to wait and see.

I let go and Dad lets go and I get my glove from the floor of the car by my feet and open the door with squeak and hop down and shut the door and wave to Dad and he waves back and I start towards home and don't look back as Dad's truck growls away until all I hear are my cleats clacking the street and the birds calling each other home for dinner.

Randy Johnson Made Me a Believer

Not in the Divine, per se, though if you watch the replay enough, the possibility becomes increasingly difficult to rule out. But more so that the universe has a devious way of putting us in our place.

Experts called it a mourning dove. Of course they did. That was part of the plan. Distract us with puns. Cosmic kamikaze disguised as avicide. An explosion of celestial feathers, beautiful if it wasn't so brutal.

The Reaper had grown too powerful. A six-ten warlock hurling flames. And so, the great bullpen in the sky threw a changeup to remind him who's in charge.

To remind us all that 2.28 is nothing compared to .00000009.

No pitch, declared the ump, with all the authority he could muster. As if he could negate a miracle. As if the very creation of a rule book was not an act of faith. He pointed to Major League Baseball Rule 8.01 (c), invoking "common sense and foul play."

No pun intended.

Was the next pitch a ball or strike? Who cares? I'll bet Randy Johnson doesn't even remember. But he damn sure got the message. Cy Youngs and ERAs and perfect games don't mean much when the groundskeeper has to clean up the mess with his bare hands, all because you waved off the curve and threw the heater, the pitch that, until a late-March afternoon, made you a baseball God.

If You're Not First,
You're Last

Looking back, the ending was obvious. The mourning doves sang, a sigh of deceit. It was summer, depression heavy in the air, heavy in our apartment, in her heavy slurps of hazelnut coffee. I hated the smell. Made my gut lurch, made my ears burn. We did not yet believe that death could come so suddenly. Not to us. Not to people like us. We went to the gym at least twice a week. We held hands at the farmer's market. People would look at us the way they do a neighbor's brand-new sedan. That's the way I imagined it. You couldn't tell me anything. I believed in registries. A light-flooded loft, crisp white brick, ample plants, faux-vintage rug on which we would fuck, because who could stop us. The kind of space that, with the right hashtag, could sear your retina.

When quarterbacks give an interview after winning the big one, they talk about God, family, the offensive line. Give thanks to all those who purchased merchandise way before they modernized the team logo. This is how I felt. Pre-ordained. It was written on her face. We were the inevitable union of hard facts, indisputable, case-closed against any sort of appeal from the wings.

All it took was a trip out of town and a smooth haircut from her past. What begins as a vibration, letters aglow on a cracked screen, ends in a quiet locker room, shaking the other team's confetti from your hair. It wasn't about feelings, she said. It wasn't about anything other than inertia. And I believed her. I believed her because she had no experience in subterfuge. I saw her phone light up one afternoon when she got up to get the cookies from the oven. His name might have been from ancient Greece, but I refuse to glorify the villain. She came back chewing a ginger snap, held out the other half, dropped it on the love-stained rug when she saw my face. There weren't tears because when you lose at the death, a trick play, a Hail Mary, there's no time to point fingers. You're on the dimmest bus ride home before the gunpowder settles on your tongue. What more can I tell you? The history books never remember second place, even if they gave us one hell of a ride, pushed the champ to the limit. It was over before I finished reading his missive, a combination

of words so obvious they made me laugh until I
began to wheeze and choke. You're scaring me, she
said, and that's when I knew I'd really loved her,
despite the bloodshed. There can be no epilogue
when you tear the final pages apart. Because death is
never a surprise ending, even when you had
promised that if either of you died first, the other
would mourn, and then find someone else to love,
whenever the timing felt right.

Drop Zone

"I feel nothing of the sort," Amy said.

We had just ridden the Drop Zone, a two-hundred-eighty-foot asshole tightener. It was her idea. I went along because that's what you do on the third date. Now we were in some low-ceilinged back room with aching white walls and fluorescence so bright you could hear it rattle.

"Your blood pressure is extremely low," said the EMT. She was heavy-set and sweet and smelled like baked bread. Her name tag said, SCARLET.

"Well, I don't know what to tell you," Amy said. "I'm fine." Her curly hair was matted to her cheek. She had sweat stains rimming her tank top. She was embarrassed. I hardly knew her. If our roles had been reversed, I would have run away. At least her puke didn't hit anyone.

"Take a few slow sips at least," Scarlet said. She handed Amy a bottle of Aquafina. Amy did as she was told. Scarlet then produced a cold compress and applied it to the small of Amy's back. Her eyes rolled up into her head and she sighed with pleasure.

"God in heaven."

It was the same thing she said after tasting good food. I had taken her to an Italian place on Prince that specialized in arancini. Crispy on the outside, chewy on the inside. Perfectly salty. An umami bomb, as the Food Network psychos would say. Amy invited me back to her place and we got undressed almost immediately. I'm no mattress hero; she told me exactly what to do with my tongue.

"You already look better," I said.

Amy opened her eyes and looked at me. She smiled. "You screamed like a girl the whole time."

Scarlet laughed. "You couldn't pay me to get on that thing."

"From the top you can see clear to Newark," I said.

"Yeah, no thank you," said Scarlet.

"Maybe we should have just waited longer," I said.

"What did you eat?"

"We split funnel cake and a milkshake," I said.

Amy puffed out her cheeks. Scarlet flinched.

"Are you—"

She retched but nothing came and there was a moment of tension, as though we'd just disarmed an explosive.

Amy looked at me again. Then she began to cry.

"Oh no," said Scarlet. "Hey, hey. It happens!"

But I knew she wasn't crying because she spewed at the apex of the Drop Zone. She was crying because her fiancé was dead. Colon cancer. Boom. Just like that. A year ago, she told me, but sometimes, out of the blue, the pain blindsided her as though it was seconds old. She was crying because this was the kind of moment you needed a partner, someone who knew you inside and out, not just the blurry birthmark on your inner thigh. I had a feeling there would be no fourth date, that this would be a tale we'd tell friends over eggs Benedict and Bloody Marys, laugh about with our future spouses on a lazy morning in bed.

"I'm so fucking stupid," Amy said, and my heart broke. She sniffed and wiped her tears with the back of her wrist, so I made a show of hustling for the box of tissues that sat next to the industrial sink.

"Thanks," she said, and blew her nose with a little honk.

"I'm going to grab you a Powerade," Scarlet said. She patted Amy on the knee then ducked out of the room.

We were alone. We were lonely. I tried to offer a smile and Amy did the same.

"Who knows," she said. "Maybe this is the spark we need."

I couldn't tell if she was joking.

"I'm still having fun," I said.

"Makes one of us."

"Your aim was impressive. Not a splash on anyone."

"You should see me on the cornhole field. Field? Pitch?"

"Sounds like a threat," I said, and Amy laughed.

Scarlet came back with an orange Powerade.

"How'd you know my flavor?" Amy said. She took the bottle and tipped it back for a long glug. "You want a taste, cowboy?"

I took the bottle and drank. It was room temperature and way too sweet.

"Tastes like Little League."

"You never told me you were an athlete," Amy said in her sultriest voice.

"How's that tummy?" Scarlet said.

I was dying to know what she thought of our relationship. If the awkwardness hung about us in a way we could never see, or if we were just another couple doing our best to hold on.

"Tummy no longer mad," Amy said. "And I bet the line for El Toro has died down by now."

Scarlet and I shared a glance.

"Kidding," Amy said. "Jesus, guys. Half my intestines are baking in the sun out there. All I want right now is my bed and a J.Lo flick."

We were quiet on the drive back to the city. Amy leaned her head against the seat as I drove. WFAN warbled low on the stereo. The Mets were down a zillion. Occasionally, I glanced over to see if she had fallen asleep. Part of me wished she would so I could be alone with my thoughts. Not that they were worth much. It's just when someone has experienced as much pain as Amy has, it gets heavy resting in the knowledge that nothing you can ever do will make it better.

"Our fair city," Amy said. "Majestic. Bold."

The skyline materialized in the haze as I sped north on the turnpike. Summer was dying, but the heat didn't get the message.

"Guess it's your turn," Amy said.

"My turn…"

"To spill your guts."

She arched her brows in a dare, then read my confusion and laughed, deep and easy.

"I'm kidding, dude. It's your turn to pick our next activity." She nodded at the radio. "Hell, I'd even let you take me to a ballgame. Have some confidence."

"I'll think on it," I said. It took everything I had not to grin like an idiot.

She patted my hand on the gear shift. "Don't hurt yourself. There's already enough pain to go around."

I drifted over to our exit. It was impossible to know if things would last. But if there was going to be pain, wasn't it worth taking a chance on a balm?

"I'll drop you off?" I said.

"If you want," Amy said. "But I wouldn't say no to company." She closed her eyes as we entered the tunnel. "At least for a little while."

Lock and Load

As it turns out, there is a wrong way to fire a machine gun. Jen had the bloody nose to prove it. The whole thing was her idea to begin with, so it was hard to feel too bad.

The evite was animated. Dancing avocados. *Dear Bach Bitches*, it read. *Get ready to channel your inner Rambo, because we're gonna shoot some shit.*

I happened to be with her when she first laid eyes on the place. We were looking for somewhere to park in the Arts District. One of Jen's coworkers, an older dude named Marco she'd slept with before she met Ben, was having an opening for his weird abstract ceramics. Jen made an illegal U-turn—sans blinker— and as she hit the turn, she looked in the rearview and said *Oh shit* in the tone reserved for cops or dropping your phone in the toilet. I stamped out my joint, but Jen said, No, stupid, machine guns. That place must be new.

I looked across the median and there it was, a low-slung concrete building painted in swirling neon colors with a giant panda stenciled on the side. He wore a camo headband tied around his fat head and an AK-47 or whatever slung around his torso. The nozzle was smoking. So was the cigarette that dangled loosely from his cartoon panda mouth.

Rad, I said, half-assed.

And when Jen said, I need to get married just to have last hurrah there, I assumed she was joking.

The place smelled like machinery and paint. The vibe was industrial chic: raw concrete floors, chrome accents, matte black ceilings to accentuate the exposed polished ductwork. In the lobby, a military helicopter was suspended from the ceiling, a massive submachine gun of some kind looming menacingly from the open door. There was even a little museum space featuring glass cases full of weapons: handguns, grenades, swords, daggers, rocket launchers, and, in the middle of the room, a deconstructed missile that, according to the little placard in clean Helvetica font, would have been deployed widely during the Vietnam War. And yet here it was, in a gentrified Miami neighborhood, in a refurbished warehouse with Pitbull bumping from the Sonos.

There were seven of us. Me, Jen, Chelsea, Ryan, Blair and the two Kates. We were given a brief tour by a guy named Pete who wore a black polo with the Panda mascot sewn into the left breast.

"Good butt," Jen whispered to me, loud enough for Pete to hear us as he led us through the small museum. He turned and smiled at me beneath the camo Dolphins ballcap that curled around his forehead.

He wasn't bad looking, strictly speaking. He was tall, solid build, a nest of brown hair spilling out the back of his cap. But he worked in *this* place. A place, it was easy to forget—what with the panda stuffies and plush cotton tees in the gift shop—that was built on death.

"Where did all this stuff *come* from?" Ryan asked. She leaned close to a glass case featuring an old brass handgun from the nineteenth century. The barrel fanned out into a horn shape, the type of thing you'd see on *Looney Tunes* that ejected a BANG! flag when you pulled the trigger.

"That's a good question," Pete said, kindly. At least he wasn't a total mansplainer. He seemed to have a genuine passion for the history of it all. "A lot of it comes from private collectors. Estate sales. Auctions. That kind of thing. You'd be surprised how many people collect this stuff."

I wasn't surprised. We were in Florida, land of football and guns and more football.

We all went for the Black Widow package, which, even at two hundred bucks a pop, was the cheapest one. The thumbnail next to the package on the LED menu behind the main counter featured a sexy red-haired femme fatale in a Lycra bodysuit holding a pistol in one hand, the other resting suggestively on her curvy hip.

"Is this the chick menu or something?" Kate S said. "If so, respectfully, fuck that."

Pete laughed behind the counter. "I don't know why they chose that graphic. You'll get plenty of brawn, trust me."

Jen insisted on paying for everyone despite our half-assed protests. She came from money—her dad was a real estate hotshot—though we never talked about it. Jen's largesse assuaged her guilt, and, as I'm sure she suspected, kept people from talking shit. *I* didn't talk shit. I didn't care who had money or where it came from. I cared about her. My beautiful, loud, hilarious, obnoxious, generous, bitchy friend, who hadn't changed since she materialized in the threshold of my freshman dorm room first week at UGA and asked if I wanted to go out and fish for some dick.

The Black Widow package included three weapons. Pete recited their names like they were items on the dinner board as he pulled them from a rack on the wall.

"First up, we've got the Heckler and Koch MP5, a German submachine gun developed in the 1960s and used in conflicts ranging from The Troubles in Ireland to the Gulf War. The variant I'm holding is semi-automatic, but the fully automatic version can fire approximately eight hundred rounds a minute."

"Fuck," I said involuntarily.

Pete laughed.

"Julie's getting all hot and bothered," Jen said. "She is *sexy*, isn't she?"

She was talking about the gun, but Pete reddened.

"And at a shade under six pounds, she's pretty sleek too. German after all."

But I wasn't reacting to the efficiency of German engineering. I was trying to understand how eight hundred bullets per minute could be needed for anything.

"Next up," Pete said, setting aside the first gun and picking up another, "We got the Spectre M4, an Italian sub developed in the mid-80s, and notably used in the Kosovar War in the '90s."

"Si si, Italiano," Kate M said. "Does it shoot Parmesan?"

Pete turned the weapon in his hands as though it might have been possible.

"Unfortunately for us, it does not. We're talking 9mm Parabellum cartridges at eight-hundred-fifty rounds per minute when fully automatic. It's a little heavier at a shade over six pounds, but it was designed for instant firepower in close combat at short ranges."

"You really know your shit, Pete," Ryan said dryly. She was the only one of us who had shot a gun before. She grew up in horse country in Virginia and so her dad, who she hated, had taught her how to shoot.

"That's why they pay me the medium-small bucks," Pete said.

Ryan smiled despite herself.

"Last, but certainly not least," Pete went on, pulling a gun off the rack that looked like something Will Smith might have used in *Independence Day*, "we have the Glock 18 submachine gun, an Austrian beauty developed in the '80s. Unlike the other weapons, this one is fully automatic."

"And it shoots one million bullets per minute," Chelsea said.

Pete humored her with a laugh. "Not quite. But nine hundred is probably more like it."

"So do we ever get to shoot the things?" Jen said, "Or you got more facts to spit, Petey."

"The bride has spoken," Pete said. "It's time."

We followed him to the range, which was divided into little booths by thin walls of smoked plexiglass. About fifty yards in front of us hung the targets, dark silhouettes in the shape of a bald man's torso, printed on heavy paper stock.

"Dark and bald," Jen said, "like Chelsea likes them."

Chelsea held up a middle finger, long and elegant. Next to it was her ring, a giant, dazzling rock that caught the dome light overhead. Her fiancé played for the Heat and Jen was jealous of the life it afforded her. Not the money per se, but the access. The travel. The prestige.

Pete ran us through the safety protocol—don't spray down the place, basically—then handed us each a set of fat cans for our ears and yellow-tinted goggles for our eyes. We looked absurd.

"We should get a pic before things get messy," I said.

"Patty Practical," Jen said, which was her way of saying good idea.

We lined up with our backs to the range, Jen in the middle, striking a leggy pose with the MP5.

"There it is," Pete said, snapping a variety of landscape and vertical. "You ladies look great."

"Take a cold shower, Petey," Jen said, and we all laughed. She leaned over and whispered in my ear. "If you don't fuck him, I will."

Ryan went first, raising the MP5 to shoulder height and widening her hips to, as Pete put it, "Establish a solid foundation." She ripped off her allotment of twenty-five bullets without any hesitation or difficulty, every pull of the trigger yielding a sharp pop, muted by our headgear. Her shoulder jerked back as though from a light shove.

"Boss bitch," Kate S said. And she was right. Ryan looked like a badass. I envied her cool confidence, that she knew exactly who she was. That the pain had become armor. When she lowered the nozzle, which actually smoked, all twenty-five rounds had struck within the concentric circles stenciled overtop the target, the majority in the inky black chest, and, as though for punctuation, one right in the forehead.

"Got ourselves a ringer," Pete said grinning.

"Only sport I'm good at," Ryan shrugged. She handed the weapon to Pete, who reloaded it expertly. Then we each took turns with the ridiculous article of death.

It was heavier than I expected. Or maybe I just had a terrible barometer for what five pounds of awkward steel was supposed to feel like. But it was intoxicating. The coy resistance of the trigger. The cool matte black metal in my hands. The little burst of fire from the nozzle. The near instantaneous clean hole that tore through the target. I hated how much I loved it.

Unfortunately, this enthusiasm didn't translate to accuracy: I was all over the damn place.

"Who'd you picture?" Ryan said as I passed the gun to Kate S.

"What?" I said.

"You gotta picture somebody," she said. "Obviously I pictured my dad. Not too hard to imagine. He's a stiff black void, just like him." She thumbed at the target. "Somebody you hate. Makes a difference. Trust me."

Truth was, I didn't *hate* anyone. I liked to think I had matured enough to where I only kept people in my life if the relationship was solid. My parents were dull, but I loved them. They wanted nothing but the best for me. My sister Candice lived in West Palm with her dentist husband and their Maltipoo, and I'm pretty sure she voted the other way, but she didn't have a mean bone in her body. Dumb maybe. But not cruel. She called me every Sunday to check on me and sent me two hundred bucks on my birthday every year. Even my ex, Chris, wasn't worthy of imaginary slaughter. He left me to go to Rabbinical school in Fort Lauderdale. We still texted each other memes from *Parks and Rec*.

I still hadn't picked someone to hate by the time it was my turn again. The Italian gun. A little heavier, but sleeker, somehow more ergonomic. A least that's the way it seemed to me.

"First time with something big and Italian in her hands," Jen said, and the girls laughed.

Pete blushed. Poor bastard. If he had to deal with groups like ours all the time, I would not blame him for clocking out and drinking heavily with the lights off.

The irony was, Jen wasn't as experienced as her bold talk would have you believe. She was raised Catholic, didn't get laid until junior year of college, and even then, it was with her boyfriend she'd begun dating at the start of sophomore year. A shy engineer named Derek who broke up with her shortly thereafter and started dating guys. Jen didn't even masturbate until she was in her mid-twenties, by which point we were living together. I even had to tell her what to do. Her first orgasm unlocked something within her though, and she went on a mini binge of men, lining up several dates a week on Hinge. But still, I couldn't help but see all the bluster as a shield, a defense mechanism to protect who I knew she really was: a shy, insecure little Catholic girl who felt competitive with me, her oldest friend, because I wasn't pre-programmed with sexual hangups and shame.

I took aim at the target and pulled the trigger. My first shot missed the target entirely. My second did too.

"It's okay hun," Jen said. "We know it's been a minute."

It was a dumb joke. A tired one. And yet as I took aim again at the target, Jen's face began to take shape within the silhouetted head. It spooked me. Her amber hair pulled back tight. The dramatic eyeliner. The thin lips. I pulled the trigger. Again. And again. And by the time I'd fired the last of my twenty-five rounds, there was a large, perforated absence near the top of the head.

"Holy cow," Pete said as he took the gun from my hands. "Somebody figured it out."

I looked at Ryan and she winked at me.

"I've had bigger," I said to Jen as Chelsea took my place in the booth. The girls laughed. Jen made a little face. I'd upstaged her. I felt a little bad. But only a little.

It wasn't my fault she was about to marry a douche. Ben was tall and good looking, sure, but he wore a perma-smirk, like he'd farted in front of you on an escalator. His family owned a chain of boutique hotels throughout the state, so he had money too. They'd met at Art Basil because of course they did. Jen said the sex was great, but I always felt she was lying. If he took the time to make her cum, I'd have been stunned. One time, I was the third wheel at a Heat game with Jen and Ben when Chelsea hooked us up with tickets. Ben sat there in his stupid loafers and berated the refs so aggressively that a member of the arena staff came by at halftime and asked him to tone it down. I was mortified.

"Boys," Jen shrugged at me with a put-upon smile. But I could see in her eyes a deep well of sadness. I wanted to take her by her exposed shoulders and shake her out of it and say, "You're the only one who expects this for yourself."

At last, it was time for the piece de resistance. The Glock 18. Pete lifted it from the little wheelie cart with a flourish and I half-expected a puff of magician's smoke.

"The one we've all been waiting for," he said.

"None of us know the difference, Pete," Kate S said.

"Oh you will when you feel it," Pete said. "And I must reiterate: please exercise added caution, because this weapon is fully automatic. It can get away from you if you're not careful. Rest the stock firmly against your armpit to absorb the additional recoil, especially on the first three to five rounds."

"Show us how it's done, RyRy," Chelsea said.

"Let's make this quick," Ryan said. "Martini time awaits and I'm getting thirsty."

She took the weapon, one that we joked about, but that had caused real damage and suffering in real circumstances we could scarcely imagine, and stepped up to the booth. She raised the stock to her shoulder and closed her left eye tight. She pulled the trigger and the short, spattering burst was almost too quick to catch. The power of it jerked Ryan's arms skyward so the spray of bullets tore a perfect vertical line in the target from navel to throat. Ryan stopped firing to collect herself.

"You weren't kidding, Petey Boy," she said.

"Got some giddy-up, don't she?" Pete said. He sounded a little nervous, as though reconsidering the life choices that had led him to this moment.

"She sure does," Jen said.

Ryan rolled her shoulders and widened her stance, nestled the gun stock more firmly in the crook of her armpit, and fired. The remaining bullets were spent in the span of a breath. The nozzle emitted a wisp of vapor and when the target at the other of the range came to rest, there was a fist-sized hole where the heart would have been.

"Nice adjustments," Pete said. He took the weapon, cocked back the slide, and handed it to Jen. She swept her copper hair over her shoulder.

"Almost sprays faster than Ben," she said.

She stepped to the target.

"Wide stance, J," Ryan said.

Jen obeyed, positioned her thin body at a three-quarter angle, her legs, which ended in Gucci loafers, shoulder-width apart. She raised the stock to her shoulder, and I wondered who, if anyone, she might have been picturing in that target. Or maybe it was blank, an abyss of confusion and fear. I felt sorry for her.

"RIP to singledom," she said, and the words had hardly left her lips by the time she had pulled the trigger for that first burst of bullets, and somehow, the stock skipped off her shoulder—maybe she had overcompensated to prevent the nozzle from rising skyward—and smashed the side of her nose. She screamed as blood immediately sprayed from her nostrils, such was the unexpected impact, and she dropped the weapon to the floor, where, by some miracle, the ensuing spray of bullets went out into the range.

We screamed. Pete sprung out to collect the weapon, engaged the safety, put it on the rack, threw his cap to the ground, took off his shirt, and balled it up to soak up the blood pouring from Jen's face. She was crying.

What struck me, more than our collective terror, was the block of text tattooed on Pete's flank. It was one of the Psalms. I couldn't catch which one.

Me and Jen were led to a white-walled side room where a member of the internal medical staff addressed Jen's nose. Her tears left streaks in the blood on her cheeks. The right side of her nose looked like a smashed strawberry. Her sobs subsided, but her shoulders jerked now and then as she tried to catch her breath. I had managed to stop crying, mostly for her sake. Her wedding was in six weeks. I knew she couldn't help but wonder what she would look like by then.

I sat next to Jen on the table and held her hand. It was clammy and cold. The nurse, a woman our age with a boyish haircut, solemnly wiped away blood with gauze.

"It's going to be okay," I said. I tried to sound convincing.

"This was all a mistake," she said. She stared out into the middle distance.

I couldn't tell if she meant the firing range or what had led to it.

"No it wasn't," I said. "Just think: this will turn into a funny story you and Ben tell for the rest of your lives."

She was quiet a moment. Her breathing slowed.

"Thank you," she said. "You're a good friend."

But I wasn't. Not anymore. And I couldn't help but wonder if she was thinking, as I was, about how the rest of your life is a very, very long time.

The Long Way

The man rolled into the lot in a dinged-up Oldsmobile. Mackey could tell right away he was trouble by the way his leather jacket hung loose about his shoulders, the tattoo that peeked from his collar. He pushed his way into the office, his hands curled into fists, and stared at Mackey until he hung up the phone.

"Can I help you?" Mackey said.

"You'd better," the man said.

Mackey thought the man was about to cry. Or had just finished.

"What's the issue?" Mackey said.

"Damn thing shudders when I hit the brakes."

"When'd it start?"

"Hell if I know. It was Ma's vehicle. Parked up her driveway for God knows how long. Told her to sell it, but she never listens. Or listened, I guess." The man cleared his throat. "Died Tuesday."

"Sorry to hear it," Mackey said. "Losing your folks is rough business."

"Did I ask you?" the man said. There was venom in his eyes.

Mackey raised his palms. "No disrespect."

"Yeah, well. Now I'm stuck with the shitbox and can't bring myself to ditch it. It's like the last I got of her. See if that makes any damn sense."

"I understand," Mackey said. "I still wear my wedding band." He held up his hand.

The air softened between them, but the man refused to allow it.

"Guess you ain't getting laid," he snorted.

"What do I call you?" Mackey said.

"Ames. Like Iowa. Where I was born at."

Mackey gave his name, held out his hand. Ames took it, squeezed hard like he had something urgent to prove, even to strangers.

"Let's take a look," Mackey said. He rounded his desk and led the way to the lot. He was confident he could fix any rust bucket you rolled over his nose. Ten years on a Winston Cup pit crew taught him cars were like math. Black and white. Absence of nuance. He liked it this way.

Customers were another thing entirely. They walked in on edge, bracing to get hosed, embarrassed they didn't know jack about transmissions and undercarriages. Especially the men. They spat out YouTube jargon—cabin air filter, main switchboard—to prove they weren't suckers. Mackey listened patiently, curiously, to lower their guard. Since Claire had died, he'd resolved to live his life in a way he hoped would make her proud, or at the very least help him understand as much about himself as he could before his cells gave out like hers did.

Ames' vehicle was a faded navy with pockmarks of rust over the wheel wells. He clocked Mackey scrutinizing it.

"Told her to keep it out of the salt air, but the garage was so full of junk you'd think she had a bead on Armageddon."

Mackey nodded in a way he hoped was sympathetic as he circled the vehicle. What he didn't say was that the man would spend more fixing it than it was worth. But reason went out the window in cases like this. People established emotional attachments to their cars like they did with pets, and sometimes went far beyond the rational. He had once done a full overhaul on a Saturn, repairs that tallied nearly ten grand, more than the car was worth off the lot, all because the woman had lost her virginity in it. Mackey had never tried therapy, but decades in the garage led him to understand the appeal.

"I'll have to keep it a day or two to get a feel for the brakes," he said.

"Figured," Ames said. He spat on the asphalt and Mackey wondered if he might start to cry again.

"Not to worry though," Mackey said. "We'll get it right."

"For the right price I bet," Ames said and crossed his arms.

"If there's one thing I pride myself on," Mackey said. He crossed his arms right back. "It's being fair."

Ames let a puff of air escape his nose, looked away. After a moment he looked back.

"I used to lie up at night wondering how it would be. Dad died when I was too young to feel it."

Mackey listened. He didn't know much, but he knew when to hold his tongue.

"You got your folks?" Ames said.

Mackey shook his head.

"Thing is, we got along good. Until we didn't. I got no brothers or sisters and she wanted grandkids. Shit, look at me. You think I'm the type? I couldn't say that to her of course. Strung it along until she could tell I was bullshitting, and that's when all our phone calls and visits petered out. Just never met the one, you know?"

Ames seemed to wait for a response, so Mackey game him one.

"It's all about timing," he said.

"Damn right it is. Spent most of my life trying to prove I wasn't no momma's boy. That I wasn't soft.

116

A man gets tired of being looked at a certain way. Teachers and wrestling coaches and all the little fucks in school knew it was just me and Ma and so they made assumptions. Those assumptions landed me in a group home for caving a kid's face in."

"You got to hold your ground," Mackey said. He detected in Ames a softness beneath all the angles, the kind Claire had coaxed out of him, especially at the end. "No one else will do it for you."

"Better believe it. Point is, when all your time is spent defending yourself, how you supposed to let a woman in?"

Despite himself, Mackey felt that in another life, he and Ames might have been friends, though something made him wonder if Ames would have wanted more than that. Not that he cared. Who you fancied was your own business. But there was a version where they'd drive out to the ridge, cast their lines in the water. Belch and tell made-up stories of their youth. Mackey would tell him about the only race his team ever won, Phoenix Raceway in '92, how he could still smell the dried beer from Victory Lane. Afterward, they'd sit side-by-side in a mildewy bar and pay half-attention to the ballgame and half-attention to the gravestone that crept up on them with each passing breath.

"Brakes ain't the only thing," Ames said. He nodded at the vehicle and Mackey was relieved they were treading back to more familiar waters. "When you first put the key in, there's a nasty buzz. Give it a listen."

Ames tossed Mackey the keys. There was a nest of them, all fastened to a keychain in the shape of a dachshund with the name COOKIE stamped below it.

Mackey opened the driver's door with a squeal. He climbed in and Ames joined him on the passenger's side. He put the key in and turned it until the lights on the dash glowed green.

"Wait for it now," Ames said and held up a finger like he was testing the wind.

Mackey waited. And waited. He realized he was holding his breath.

"Want me to cut it off and on again?"

"Shh," Ames said, so they waited some more.

Mackey could smell the man now that they were in the stuffy Olds interior. He could smell his sweat over the stale cigarette odor that was by now baked into the maroon fabric seats. Mackey nearly asked Ames if it was lung cancer, the same thing that killed Claire, but he stopped himself.

"Christ," Ames said. He slapped the door panel with an open palm. "Just did it this morning. Nasty buzz. Like a rattle."

"That's the way it goes," Mackey said. "But I know what you mean. If it happens again, I'll hear it. And I'll go ahead and bump you to the front of the line."

"Hell, you'd do that?" Ames said. His voice wavered and Mackey started to wonder if there was even an issue with the breaks. Or if Ames had lost the only person he had in this world and so he had set out in search of something to fill the void. Someone neutral to listen, to hold his burden, even for a few minutes.

"Sometimes a car isn't just a car," Mackey said.

Ames nodded. He idly reached over and clicked on the radio, scanned the dial through blips and static, snatches of a Dolly song Mackey couldn't place, then clicked it off.

"I know this thing ain't worth fixing in the first place."

"We can work all that out," Mackey said, and he meant it.

"That's not what I mean," Ames said. "Look, what do you say we just drive for a little while. Don't matter where. Pick a direction. Then I'll go on my way."

Mackey was quiet a moment as he thought about it. His breath whistled from his nostrils.

"What?" Ames said with an edge. "You think I'm some creep or something? You don't know shit." But just as he reached for the door handle, Mackey surprised himself by firing the engine and putting the car in gear.

Sometimes, he figured, what you had to give was your time and that was enough.

"About lunch time anyway," he said.

"I guess it is," Ames said. His shoulders settled. He leaned back against the headrest and closed his eyes.

"I know a place," Mackey said. "Burgers and shakes."

"Fine by me," Ames said. His eyes were still closed. He exhaled, slow and deep, as though finally setting something down. "Do me a favor and take the long way."

Mackey led them out of the lot, flipped the clunking blinker and turned onto the byroad. The long way was just fine with him. It had led the two of them to very different conclusions and yet here they sat together. Sure, Mackey thought, the long way would do. It was the only way as far as he was concerned.

What Gouda Knew

Maggie had ended up with Gouda. She didn't choose him. He didn't choose her. He was a Scottish fold—an expensive, sought-after breed—which Maggie only knew because she took a photo of the animal's smushed face and uploaded it to Google.

When Bryce, Maggie's twin, was dying, one of the last things she said to Maggie was, *Take care of Gouda. He loves whipped cream, but don't give him too much. He'll get fat.*

Get? Gouda already looked like a toad. Maggie didn't say this to her dying sister, of course. What she said was, *Me?*

Meaning: You really trust me to keep something alive? Have you seen where I live? I barely know how to scramble an egg.

Bryce didn't even have the chance to answer. The monitors next to her hospital bed began to frantically bleep and bloop until a squadron of nurses and aides rushed in and boxed Maggie out.

It wasn't the last time Maggie saw her sister. That wouldn't come for a few more months. But Bryce was so weakened by then the only thing she could manage to say was I love you in a voice so papery

Maggie had to put her ear to her sister's lips just to hear it.

And then she was gone.

An autoimmune condition. Ultra rare according to the pamphlets. Something about blood platelets. She was twenty-eight. Maggie was twenty-eight too. Now an only child to parents who collapsed so fantastically into grief that Maggie hadn't even seen them since the funeral.

Gouda came home with her in a foam crate. At first, he was skeptical. He would sit by the sliding glass door and stare blankly at the yard. He refused to eat, even though Maggie bought the exact brand of organic slop that Bryce had instructed. He expressed total disinterest in the squishy softball toy Maggie had bought for him at the H-E-B and ignored the Cool Whip she set out in a little Astros helmet.

The hell is wrong with you? Maggie would say. Do something. Be a cat.

But she knew deep down. She knew because she felt the same way most of the time: Gouda was depressed.

After a particularly concerning week during which Gouda slept about twenty hours a day, snoring loudly through his smushed face, Maggie sat down to do research, scouring cat subreddits where the posts often frightened her. Who were these people? Posting about cat sushi. About cat IVF. The man in South Dakota who ran a cat farm. Three hundred tabbies on a twenty-acre plot. Who *were* these people. Until one post caught her eye. In familiar staccato sentences, a user explained how she was living with a terminal disease. She didn't have long. She had a beloved Scottish Fold.

Maggie's heart raced as she leaned in and read the post.

The redditor's fiancé would be too heartbroken. She was thinking about putting her cat up for adoption. But she hated the idea of the animal going to a strange home. She had a twin. Maybe her sister could adopt the cat? Trouble was, as much as she loved her sister, she was immature. Irresponsible. Lived alone. Had no partner and few friends. Would she be capable? Any advice?

Was this what Bryce really thought of her? Of course it was. She had no reason to lie in an anonymous forum under the name CheeseMama3280. And it was hard to argue. Maggie couldn't have been more different from her twin. They weren't best friends or joined at the hip like every other set of twins Maggie knew. Bryce was an overachiever. High school salutatorian. Peace Corps. A rising star at a non-profit focused on clean water in at-risk communities. Engaged to a perfectly boring blonde guy named Rick who worked for Liberty Mutual.

Maggie barely knew what she wanted for lunch, let alone in life. Or in a partner for that matter. In college—a different school to avoid the inevitable comparisons to her twin—at least there had been structure. She played softball: good enough for a scholarship, not good enough to start. But it was an identity, and she hadn't been prepared for what would happen when the final whistle blew. Since then, she'd bounced from temp job to temp job, a series of increasingly depressing and horrifically-lit cubicle farms. Answering phones for a local law firm, selling tickets for Monster Jam, and ironically, data entry for the ASPCA. For Maggie, choosing one thing meant closing the door on hundreds of possibilities. She'd rather be unsure than wrong.

Maggie scanned the replies to Bryce's post, heartbroken.

Cats are easy…if your sister can't figure out how to take care of one, she's a sociopath.

Sounds risky. Seems like your sister needs therapy, not an animal.

Maggie began to cry, harder and harder until her eyes blurred and the words on her screen swam together. Despite their differences, losing Bryce was like losing a part of herself. She was a twin. She was an athlete. Now she was neither.

She felt something brush her leg. She wiped her eyes on the sleeve of her hoodie and looked down to find Gouda looking up at her with those big dumb alien eyes, holding the softball in his mouth. One of his nubby ears twitched.

What do you want? Maggie said. Go away.

She nudged his flank with her socked foot, but Gouda didn't move. He set down the softball toy, blinked at her slowly, then let out a short, stuttering meow that sounded like he was trying to say *brown.*

What! Maggie said. I'm not Bryce, dummy!

Gouda patiently sat on his haunches. He continued to stare at her. He pawed her shin.

Brown? he said.

Ugh! Maggie said. *Now* you want to hang out?

Despite herself, Maggie reached down and lifted Gouda by the belly. His stubby legs dangled in the air. His expression was unchanged. Dumb as a brick.

She put him in her lap, feeling his bulky warmth. A warmth Bryce must have felt hundreds of times.

Okay, Maggie said to the animal. Now what?

Gouda stood in her lap, then padded a little circle until he was satisfied that, Yes, this lap would suffice, and then he collapsed heavily onto Maggie's thighs. An ash-grey shrimp. A furry croissant.

He licked her thumb.

That did it.

Maggie began to cry again, even harder now, sobs that wracked her shoulders, rocked Gouda's doughy body where he lay. He continued to lick Maggie's hand, his little tongue pink and papery.

With her other hand, Maggie stroked his head. He let her do it. She brushed the fur between his weird ears. She bent over and kissed his soft head, surprising herself. He let her do that too.

Gradually, the tears subsided, and when they did, Gouda stopped licking her hand. He closed his bug eyes and fell asleep.

Guess we're stuck here, Maggie said to the sleeping lump.

She reached out to shut her laptop when a comment caught her eye.

Maybe, the comment read, *you guys are missing the point. Maybe the point is that he will take care of her.*

The Neon Surfer

The surfer paddled out in a neon wetsuit—Day-Glo green, complete with booties and hood—a human highlighter in the drift. We couldn't tell if it was a woman or a man. I sat on my board next to Ray—an HVAC repairman who'd been surfing this break since he was a boy—our feet dangling in the water as we waited for a set that might never come.

"Wonder what the fish think," Ray said as we watched the surfer paddle brightly by.

"Makes rescue easy, I guess," I said.

Don't get me wrong, the bromides you hear about surfers are true. The childlike wonder of catching a wave, the beauty of the ocean. The serenity. The unpredictability of it all, a gentle reminder to carry patience with you out of the water and into your life. But really, I loved going out for moments like the one I shared with Ray: aimless, in-between, just two mediocre surfers with mediocre lives sharing a moment in the water. We were both divorcees. I caught my wife cheating with our daughter's karate instructor—our daughter, who I got to see twice a month. As boring and as mortifying as it gets. Ray struggled with booze. It took his wife of twenty-one years leaving him for him to go to AA and find some form of God. "Not blue-eyed Jesus," he told me once as we waxed our boards before a session, "but this." He gestured broadly with his arm and looked out at the horizon. It was an ugly day, metallic and heavy and humid. For a moment, I thought he was going to cry. "It's wasted on us, ain't it?"

We watched now as the neon surfer paddled east in the direction of the rock jetty that protruded crudely from shore.

"Must know something we don't," Ray said.

It had always been a dead spot, something about depth and crosscurrents I didn't fully grasp. But sure enough, within moments, a set rolled in, and me and Ray and the two other guys in the water nearby looked on as the surfer positioned themselves perpendicular to the horizon, looked over their shoulder, and waited for the precise moment to begin paddling toward shore, until a four-footer began to crest and the neon surfer, a woman, I could see that now, pushed herself up on her board, an eight-foot twin-fin with black piping. With balletic grace at odds with both her age and her garish wetsuit, she carved her way westward.

"Well fudge me," Ray said. "First time for everything."

As the woman paddled back out, Ray shouted to her.

"How did you know? I've been surfing this break since Reagan and never seen nothing over there."

The woman smiled at us as she paddled.

"I'm old," she said.

And she was. Her weathered face—poking through her Lycra hood—was wrinkled and squished.

"Show us the way," Ray said.

"More fun if you make your own," she said, then she maneuvered her board about fifty yards beyond our spot in the water.

"Seen her out here before?" I said.

"No sir," Ray said. "Maybe she usually comes out when the rest of us don't bother."

Outside of Ray, I hadn't made much of an effort to get to know any of the other regulars. There was the young guy with the straggly bleached hair who always rolled up in a doorless jeep blasting Dead Kennedys. He rode a short board and surfed violently, as though trying to teach the ocean a lesson. There was the mother and her tween daughter, who both rode foam tops and laughed infectiously as they teetered and flailed and tipped over into the froth. The girl reminded me of Izzy. I don't know what my ex fed her about me—that I was a loser probably, that I never tried hard enough, that after my novel didn't sell, I fell into a deep depression and forgot how to live. If it wasn't so cliché, I would've felt sorry for myself. But when even your pain is crushingly average, you start to see the humor in it. What hurts the most is that Izzy doesn't seem to know how to behave around me. She isn't glued to her phone like the other girls her age. It's more that she becomes passive and withdrawn and quiet, acquiescing to whatever dumb plan I have for our days together, as though she doesn't want to hurt me anymore than Janet already has. The silver lining is that the last time I saw Iz, she told me she quit karate because Carl was a shitty instructor. Plus he had salami breath. I had to keep myself from jumping up on the table at Baskin-Robbins. On the few occasions Ray and I have dipped a toe in water of vulnerability, he's told me I'm lucky to have a kid at all. "She never wanted one," he told me once. "What could I do but respect it?" I could see the hurt in his eyes as he spoke, right before he paddled into a rolling three-footer and rode it to shore, and we never brought it up again.

"Hold the phone," Ray said, and sure enough, a small set rolled in where the neon surfer had positioned herself. Again, we watched as she waited patiently for the perfect moment, paddled, pushed herself up, and elegantly maneuvered her board, her feet moving with a delicate precision as though tiptoeing a creaky floor, and she rode the wave for what seemed like an eternity. It was one of the most beautiful things I'd ever seen.

Wordlessly, Ray and I turned to each other, and soon we were paddling over to where the neon surfer arranged herself next.

"Don't let us crowd you," I said, but she batted the comment away.

"Plenty for everyone," she said. "That's the beauty."

There were many surfers who would disagree, who turned the platonic ideal of the mellow surfer—spiritual and free—into its edgy, competitive, territorial opposite. I was not one of them. Neither was Ray. But maybe that was my problem. Maybe if I had been more like Karate Carl, I'd still have my family.

"She's done it again," Ray said, and we watched as a set of gentle waves emerged from beyond.

"Go get it partner," I said. I looked at our companion as though for permission. She smiled and nodded.

Ray squared himself on his board and paddled into a wave that produced a foamy spray at its lip. His mechanics seemed to defy the laws of physics: his keg-like torso and matchstick legs made him top-heavy, so he had to stoop at the waist to keep his balance. But he did, maneuvering his body to get the most out of it, like an old car with which you develop a compassionate shorthand.

"There he goes," the neon surfer said as Ray pumped his skinny legs to keep momentum on his ride. Her voice was infused with the kind of quiet joy that takes a lifetime to earn. I wanted to ask her questions. Where was she from? How was she able to read the ocean with such freaky accuracy? What should I do with the rest of my life? What I said instead was, "Where did you nab that suit?"

The neon surfer looked at me as a bead of water dripped from her nose and caught the sun. "It was my daughter's," she said. Then she gestured toward the horizon at a perfect wave heading right at us. "If you don't take that, I will."

So I did what I was meant to do. I accepted her generosity and paddled into position, and at the precise moment, as the wave rolled beneath my board, I pushed myself up, feeling the effortless momentum, as though the ocean was carrying me in its arms, the water below me glancing by, the thrill in my gut that never goes away, never gets old, and it was in that moment I knew I would bring Izzy with me next time, like my dad once brought me. She would protest—*So boring!*—and no doubt get frustrated for her first few attempts, but with a little persistence, some soft coaching, and a modicum of faith, she would catch her first wave, a moment she'd remember for the rest of her life.

The wave carried me nearly to shore, a few hundred yards from where I'd caught it. I paddled back out, scanned the horizon, and spotted Ray's bulky upper body bobbing atop his board. The sun dipped behind a band of clouds causing one of those instantaneous drops in temperature. I shivered.

I rejoined Ray where he sat and looked around for the neon surfer.

"Where'd she go?" I said.

Ray shrugged. "Beats me. Must've gone in while we were joyriding. Or maybe she went off to another break we've never even dreamed of."

I looked about, hoping I might spot her.

"Bummer," I said. "I wanted to thank her."

"For what?" Ray said, pushing his thin hair back on his forehead.

As I thought about my answer, the clouds broke and the sun shone through, and I was blinded by the glitter and spark of the chop.

"For making space," I said.

Man Up

Mom had a closed casket, so Coach was the closest I'd ever been to death. I don't care what anyone says. Seeing a dead body, especially one that was as alive as his was just seconds before—sweating, stomping, hollering, *alive*—will fuck you all the way up.

He was gone by the time his head smacked the parquet. His face looked like a sweaty pizza left in the sun. For a moment, play went on, and the crowd roared as Ty swished a jumper from the elbow to cut our deficit to six. I was at the scorer's table getting ready to check back in, so I was right there when it happened. I mean, *right there*. I was supposed to go back in and take over. Coach had been letting me cook—run the offense, take the heat. All part of the plan: play hard, get good looks, score in bunches. Keep showing the world I was League-ready. Me, the local white boy with the smooth jumper and a lottery-grade first step. Get to the next level. Set up a life. For me and Alaina. Get her mom out of that apartment. Get Dad into a place with actual drywall. Just get us all to the next phase.

Kat, our team doctor, scrambled onto the court when it became clear Coach wasn't moving. Clemson's point guard picked up his dribble, took out his mouth guard and pointed. Play stopped. A murmur bubbled through the arena. Kat tried CPR. Puffed out his ruddy cheeks with her own frantic breath. *Puff. Puff. Puff.* Compressing his chest with violent shoves that racked his doughy body.

"Get up, Coach!" Ty shrieked. But it was obvious. The frozen hollow look in his eyes, glaring up into nothing. Soon, the twelve thousand faces in the hushed arena knew it too. Kat sat back on her haunches and took Coach's pulse with two fingers on his wrist. Then she looked around at our huddle of faces peering down at the scene and shook her head. The crowd was so quiet you could hear the humming ductwork in the cavernous rafters where all the old banners hung.

The head ref, the bald fuck that gave me a bullshit technical in the first half for arguing a call, screeched his whistle so loud I can still feel it scrape the roof of my skull when my brain is on fire and the insomnia is at its worst. He waved his hands in a flourish. "That's it," he said. "Ballgame."

Never made it up either. Ten minutes left in the second half. Down six at home to the worst team in the conference. If we'd played like we were supposed to, Coach might still be alive. And my life might look a whole lot different.

The locker room was silent. The fifteen of us sat at the sleek wooden cubbies that bore our last name and jersey number. I stared at the carpet, the giant team logo stamped in the plush. The fuck were we supposed to do now? Banks was crying, trying to hide it with a towel. Six-eleven, two-ninety, sniveling like a little kid. Last I heard he was playing pro ball in Taiwan. If he ever cried like that at the next level? He'd never touch the rock. There's a narrative about how toxic masculinity is changing in sports, but nah, not really. It's kill or be killed. Always has been. Always will be.

Coach Bishop was pacing the middle of our circle. Rubbing his stubble. Realizing it was his ship now. Trying to figure out how hot to come in, how soon. I looked over at Ty. He'd already dug his phone out of his blood-red team-issued duffle and was scrolling the reactions on his feed. I caught his eye, tried to tell him to ditch it, the same type of ESP we had on the court. He looked away.

"Put the fucking device away Gilchrist," Bishop barked. Ty jumped, did as he was told.

"This was a shock," Bishop rasped, quieter now. "What is there to say? He was a good Coach. Even better man." He made a point of looking each of us in the eye. Practicing for the press conference, the quotes that would get shared on IG. "Never take this game for granted. Okay? This is your team. This is your life. For the rest of the season, we're like this," he made a tight fist. "One unit. One goal." He paused. "One heart. You hear me?" Another pause. Banks blew snot into his towel. "I said, do you *hear me, goddamn it?*"

"YEAH," we all said.

It was surreal. What was any of this for?

"Good." Bishop bowed his head. "A moment of silence. For Coach."

We obeyed. I snuck a look around. Most of the guys had their eyes shut. Givens. Monk. Watts. Banks' chin still quivering. I looked over at Ty, caught his eye again. He looked scared. I looked away.

"Okay," Bishop said, took a deep breath. "Bring it in."

We got up off our stools and put our hands— still sweaty from a game the record books say never even happened—in the middle of the circle.

"Coach on three," Bishop said, his voice low, setting the stage for the unified boom. "One...two...*three...*"

We showered. We dressed. We packed our shit. We cleared our throats. We hugged self-consciously, hardly looking each other in the eye. We left. All in near silence. It felt like the end of the season even though we had two weeks to go and the tournament on top of that. If we even made it that far.

Me and Ty sat in his truck and smoked a blunt. *It's Dark and Hell is Hot* played on the stereo linked through his phone. "Damien," the one where DMX raps a conversation with the Antichrist. Ty's brother put him onto all the old-school nineties shit. X, Wu-Tang, Nas, Big Pun. His room at his one-bedroom off-campus was papered in old covers of *The Source*.

"You think they cancel the season?" he said. Blunt smoke hovered and curled around his short braids. We were parked way out by the soccer fields under a streetlamp, about as far away as you could get and still be in the arena lot.

"You serious?" I said. I pinched the dwindling blunt from his fingers. The embers singed my skin. "No chance. You heard Bishop. We'll take a game off. *Maybe.* The school has too much to lose. Like, marketing and shit. Especially with the tourney coming up."

Ty nodded, leaned back in the driver's seat. I could never tell how depressed he really was.

"Fucking Coach," he said. "They really put a sheet on him and wheeled his ass out."

"Feel like that's how he would've wanted to go," I said through smoke.

"On a gurney?"

"On the court. No wife. No kids. Hoop was his life."

"Dying on ESPN2? Shit, sad as hell."

"Tragic maybe," I said, "but not sad. The tribute videos are already flowing."

"Hey," Ty said. "*HEY.*" He pitched his voice down to sandpaper levels, just barely above Phil Jackson on the scale of torched vocals.

"Chill," I said and grinned.

He jutted his chin way out to mimic Coach's underbite.

"Listen. Fellas. We get *back on D*. We foul *hard*. We get a *win*. We get *laid.*"

I choked on a laugh, passed back the blunt. Bass rattled the loose change in the cupholders. The truck, courtesy of a rich alum who hooked it up on the sly before the NIL deals went crazy, was all black inside and out. Ty called it The Hearse.

"*Tyson*," I said. My impression sucked compared to his, but this was our game. "Ask not what your teammates can do for you—"

"Ask what *you* can do for your teammates," Ty rasped.

We cackled together and then we were quiet. We didn't know how to mourn, especially not in front of one another.

"Fucking Coach," I said.

"Damien" faded out. "How's It Goin' Down" faded up.

Ty exhaled heavy. I knew what he was thinking. He pulled on the blunt and the cherry glowed in the dim cocoon.

"Bishop finally getting his shot," he said.

"If he wasn't such an asshole maybe he would've got it already."

"Fucking Coach," Ty said.

Coach is—*was*—a player's coach. Didn't run us into the ground. Didn't care if we smoked weed. As long as we were ready to play and we played hard and didn't fail a drug test. He knew what was up. He knew what it took to get to the next level because he almost got there, was an Achilles tear away from serious NBA looks. You wouldn't have known it by the bowling ball gut under his shirt, but he was on the Utah squad that went to the chip in the late-nineties. One of the only non-Mormons. An outsider. I think that's why me and him were tight.

Ty clicked back on his phone and "Get At Me Dog" leapt from the speakers.

"Again?"

Ty pumped-faked with the blunt, held it out of reach. "Sorry pardner," he said, putting on his Dave Chappelle white guy voice. "No Jack Johnson on this here mow-bile phone."

"Fuck you," I said. I snatched the roach. "Bet you the rest of this bag Bishop dials up his regimen in the first practice back."

"Sucker's bet," Ty said. He's gonna run us til we puke. Just to prove a point. Just to—oh *shit*."

Ty looked past me out the passenger window just as a fist pounded on the glass. I jumped, dropped the roach, felt the cherry burn my ankle and tried to stamp it out.

"Watch the fucking mat, champ," Ty said. The fist pounded again.

"I gotta open it."

"Don't," Ty said, but I was already pressing the window button. The February air spilled in as smoke spilled out. Peering at us was a face we knew. Jacobs. School security. Hoop fan. Mega nerd. Turned a blind eye when he would catch us breaking into the gym late nights to get shots up, but only because we let him hang and hooked him up with tickets.

"You boys okay?" Jacobs said. He leaned his moony face into the window and sniffed. His doughy cheeks were pink in the cold. "Smells like a party."

"More like a wake," I said, turning down the stereo.

Jacobs shook his head gravely. "I still can't believe it. Heavy stuff."

"We good," Ty said. He was high as fuck. Eyes like wet marbles.

Jacobs nodded. "I can see that."

"You want some?" I said. It was worth a shot.

"Marijuana?" Jacobs said. Ty stifled a giggle. "Appreciate the invite, but no can do. I gotta whizz in a cup once a month."

"Fucked up," Ty croaked.

"Yeah, well. I suppose we all got responsibilities," Jacobs said. "You boys can keep this party going, but you can't do it here, okay?"

"Loud and clear," I said. Ty swallowed back more laughter.

"Sorry about Coach," Jacobs said. He popped his open palm on the lip of the window. "He was always real kind to me."

Ty dropped me off at Alaina's apartment off Sterling. She answered the door in one of my team hoodies. It fell over her hands and almost to her knees. I could tell she had nothing underneath.

"C'mere," she said. I stepped inside and she squeezed me hard. I cradled her head against my collarbone, kissed the top of her scalp, which smelled like coconut. She'd just showered. "I'm so sorry," she was saying. "Everyone's texting me." She nodded to the TV in the corner. SportsCenter was on. "They've been running tributes."

On the screen, the bland anchor was speaking solemnly about Coach, about how he got his start at a high school deep in Brooklyn where he won and just kept on winning. About how he got hired as an assistant as a mid-major program in Missouri, and when that coach was fired, he became the interim head coach and quickly turned them around from perennial nothinghood into a respected squad that, in only his third year at the helm, made it to their first NCAA tournament in sixty years. About how, ten years ago, he was hired at Mountain Ridge, a blue-blood program in the dumps, glory days long gone, and once again worked his magic, convinced kids from New York City and Los Angeles and Dallas and Chicago to take a chance on him, to come to a little college town in the mid-Atlantic, and returned the program to respectability, and to then back-to-back Final Fours, the second of which was my freshman year. *Sadly*, the anchor said, *He never did get a chance to cut down the nets.*

As he spoke, subtitles unspooled at the bottom edge of the screen. Hovering over the anchor's left shoulder was a photo of Coach. Younger. Healthier. Happier. I couldn't take it. I picked up the remote from the couch and hit the button. The anchor vanished into the mirrored void.

"You don't want to see?" Alaina said.

"I already saw," I said, and she looked at me with real concern, so I went to the fridge and got a beer.

I sat on the couch. Alaina jammed her icy feet beneath my thighs for warmth. I was right: nothing beneath the sweatshirt.

"Talk to me," she said.

When it came to feelings and shit, I wasn't much of a talker. What was the point? Why dump your garbage on someone else? Mom always tried to tell me I could be vulnerable and still be a competitor. "Look at me," she'd say. "I can drop thirty on the Sparks and still come home to kiss you goodnight." But when she passed, that part of me became harder to access.

"I'm gonna miss him," I said. "We all are. I mean, he took a chance on me. A local white boy."

"You're more than that," Alaina said. Her face softened. She was worried about me.

"I love you," I said. I didn't say it enough.

"I love you too, baby," she said.

When I would tell people about Alaina— scouts, boosters, alumni—they'd give me a look like, *Be careful.* But they didn't know. They didn't know she was with me when I was nobody. Sophomore year of high school, five-foot-five, couldn't even touch the rim. Just a kid with a busted jumper and a dead mom. The vultures, they're the ones who want something from me, not Alaina. She didn't care if I got to the league or wound up coaching back at Lincoln. She just wanted me—us—to be happy.

"How's Ty?" she was saying.

I shrugged. "He's Ty."

What was I supposed to say? That my gut told me he was deeply sad, but didn't have the vocabulary, or confidence, really, to express it? That NBA scouts questioned a place in the league for a guard his size? That he wasn't strong enough to guard the pick and roll? That his father drifted back into his life in the hopes the scouts were wrong? That he self-medicated by getting so high he could barely speak? I couldn't say it because to put it in the ether meant I would have to figure out what to do about it.

Instead, I reached my hand into the open hem of Alaina's sweatshirt.

"Careful," she said, gently chastising. She bit her bottom lip, tilted her head back.

She sat up, swung her legs over and straddled me, put her hands in the air. I slid the hoodie off and threw it to the floor. I ran my hands over her body, her smooth torso, the butterfly tattoo on her flank that had been there since we met, that honored her little sister who drowned when Alaina was ten. I guess pain attracts pain.

She kissed me hard, tasting like nicotine. She'd snuck one even though she knew I hated it. She pulled off my sweatshirt and t-shirt. I hoisted her up, her legs cinched tight around my waist, and carried her to the bedroom. I loved that shit. We didn't even make it to the bed or turn on music or turn off the lights, we just fucked right there on the rug at the foot of her bed, the one with the leafy patterns on it that Alaina's grandmother gave her. Her roommate Courtney was at her boyfriend's, so we could be as loud as we wanted. Alaina on her back, then me behind her, then her on top, the little hoop piercing through her left nipple bouncing as she worked her hips, until we were both collapsed together, a sweaty pretzel of arms and legs.

"Is it always this good when somebody dies?" Alaina said.

And we laughed, but looking back, that might've been one of the last times we laughed together before the heaviness descended. What neither of us knew was that it was something like an omen. But right then, it was a joke, a dark one, and Alaina kissed her fingers and touched her tattoo. "Sorry sis," she said.

I took a piss and brushed my teeth while Alaina moved the scrum of stuffed animals and pillows off the bed, the blue elephant she'd had since she was a girl, the little owl I got her at the airport on a road swing through the Pacific Northwest that she named Carl. On nights when I didn't stay over, she slept with Carl tucked under her chin. That killed me, made me want to do everything I could to take care of her. Not that she needed any protecting. She was tough. Pulling your sister's body out of a lake on what was supposed to be a family vacation will do that to you. After Cami drowned, her parents couldn't take it, so they split. Her dad went off the deep end and moved to a trailer in a marina in

Virginia Beach surrounded by nothing but gravel and rust and red-pilled Facebook shitposts. Her mom called once a week pretending everything was fine. You'd never know it though. Alaina was the smartest woman I'd ever met. Business/Psych double major, already auditing some MBA classes. Her plan was to start a brand of gyms geared toward women—men could come too if they wanted—that was affordable and approachable to all shapes and sizes, and, as Alaina put it, warm. Not cunty and psycho like the cycling and bootcamp cults, she'd say. She had a vision. I believed in her.

She took my place in the bathroom and left the door cracked while she peed. I could see her underwear around her ankles, the chipped white paint on her toes. It always made me laugh, the sound of it, like you were squeezing a water bottle as hard as you could.

"Shut up," she said, unspooling toilet paper. "You are such a child."

"You got a strong core."

"I'd kick your ass."

"I know."

"When are we getting married?" she said over the flush of the toilet.

"After," I said. I picked up a heavy copy of *Vogue* from her nightstand and flipped through a kaleidoscope of ads and gaunt women and nauseatingly sweet perfume.

Alaina was quiet. We spoke about the draft indirectly so we didn't fuck around and jinx it. I still hadn't signed with an agent, but the chatter was that I was a lottery pick, top twelve, guaranteed money.

"Promise?" She clicked on her electric toothbrush and stood leaning against the door jamb in an XL tee I once caught at a Wizards game. Her hair was up in a bun and I started to get hard again. She looked so hot when her guard was down.

"Don't look at me like that," she said through toothpaste foam. Some fell from her chin and onto the carpet. She rubbed it in with her foot.

I laughed. She gave me the finger. I laughed harder. She ducked back into the bathroom and spit.

"You fucking promise?"

"I promise," I said. "We're going to be the most married assholes ever to marry."

"That's what I'm talking about."

I tossed the magazine onto the floor and propped myself on an elbow to watch her sit cross-legged on the bed, cleaning her face with these eucalyptus face wipes, applying her moisturizing cream in well-practiced circles. Her phone was next to her open to TikTok, sweeping drone videos of Icelandic waterfalls.

"I'll take you there someday," I said.

"Come here," she said.

I leaned in and closed my eyes and she put some of the cream on the space between my eyebrows.

"Rub it in."

"You do it."

She kissed her teeth. "You are such a child."

"That's cause I never got to be one."

She rubbed the cool cream into my forehead with gentle force.

"Boo hoo," she said. Then she kissed me where the cream had been because she knew I meant it.

We got under the covers and Alaina snuggled close, rested her head on my chest. It was our routine. She was a heavy sleeper, could knock out anytime, anywhere, a survival mechanism from a childhood shuttling around from place to place with her mom, car rides back and forth to DC to stay with her grandma while her mom tried to make it with new men. It never worked out, but Alaina protected herself by sleeping through it.

I picked up my phone to scroll, trying to wind down before I killed the light, but I knew what I was getting myself into. As soon as I opened my feed, it blew up with red alert notifications, DMs, comments. The algorithm flooded my feed with photos and videos of Coach. From our Sweet Sixteen run last year. From his early coaching days, when he was slim, fresh-faced, and young, not much older than me. Reporters hitting me up for comments, fans sending condolences, creeps asking me if it was staged. College basketball was already a life in a fishbowl, and now it seemed like there were more faces than ever peering in.

Alaina rubbed my chest. She must have felt that I'd been holding my breath.

"It's gonna be okay," she said, sleepily. I couldn't see her hazel eyes, but I knew they were closed, that she was moments away from sleep.

"I know," I said, and it's possible in that moment I believed it.

I clicked off the bedside lamp and put my phone on the nightstand. Alaina kissed me on the cheek and rolled over and within seconds, her breathing was deep and even. Now and then her foot twitched.

I envied her. That sleep could come so easily and deeply.

It usually started with a simple statement that floated up into my brain like a viscous object: *I'm not going to sleep tonight.* Occasionally, there were nights where I would have some trouble falling asleep, tossing and turning for an hour or two until consciousness slipped softly away at last. Nights before big games. The first night of a stretch on the road. Nervous excitement and jittery restlessness, a buzz and hum beneath the surface of my skin, like how I'd felt the night before Christmas as a kid, back before Mom died.

But this felt different. My body knew something before my brain did. It was a bottomless pool, deep and dark. A late-night radio tuned to the wrong frequency.

I tossed and turned, as lightly as I could so I wouldn't wake Alaina, even though she could sleep through an earthquake. I needed rest. Blackout. A break. A clean eight hours. But wanting it only pushed it away. And I just couldn't stop thinking about Coach, picturing his twisted vacant face, his dead eyes open, a thousand-yard stare, like he was looking up past the huddled faces shouting his name in vain, looking up through the domed roof of the arena, into the sky and beyond, the abyss we'd all see someday, but never talk about.

Coach was always honest with me. Never promised me playing time. Never gassed me up. But when he was recruiting me, he told me if I wanted to be a part of something bigger than myself, if I wanted to be ready for the next level, there was only one place to play. And he was right. I never told him I made my decision because it's where Mom went, where I could carry on her name. Coach believed in me, and I wanted him to know I believed in him. And I never told him thank you. He put the ball in my hands and gave me a green light. As a freshman. Unheard of. *If it feels like leather, shoot it.* That's what he said. He came to my home, the apartment Dad is still in, sat down on our ratty-ass couch with the foam exposed, his team-issued golf shirt buttoned to the top, sweating because our AC was busted. He looked Dad in the face and said he could help turn me into a good man, and, if I really wanted it, a wealthy one. That's all Dad needed to hear. When Coach left, Dad poured himself a gin, leaned against the sink and said, "I believe him." Which surprised me. Because I expected him to talk about how the game took Mom away from us and this huckster with the big red face better not take me away too. I always said it was the heart attack that took Mom away and Dad would say, "You know what I mean." And I did.

On my official visit, I toured the facilities: the locker room—pristine and gleaming—the weight room with all its brand-new machines, and the arena with a dozen jerseys in the rafters bearing famous names from long ago. The arena where Coach would ultimately spend his last seconds on this earth. They even had a jersey printed up for me with my name stitched on the back, number eleven, which they knew I wore in honor of Mom.

After all the pomp and circumstance, a few of the guys took me out to the bars just off campus where we didn't pay for a damn thing. I might as well have been rolling with Steph and LeBron. The starting center at the time, a junior and a projected top-five pick that summer, was surrounded by women wherever he went, and at one point disappeared to the bathroom of a bar called Trinity with two blondes that barely reached his chest. When he came back and the two girls were wiping their mouths, the rest of the guys barely flinched.

From there we took an Uber to a strip club called the Paper Moon about twenty minutes away and the center pulled a fistful of dollar bills from the pocket of his jeans and sprayed them around the stage as a tattooed woman with platinum high heels and fake tits writhed and swung around the pole. It was clear this was a regular thing. I always hated strip clubs. The desperation. The sticky floors. The cloying sweetness of the perfume. The glitter that sticks to your clothes even after a wash. The terrible fucking ten songs that never leave the stereo. But that night I rolled with it because what else was I supposed to do? Politely excuse myself? Raise objections to the dead-eyed stares my future teammates fixed on the stage as a young woman our age slapped her ass and licked her lips and whipped her hair around? You do what you need to do to fit in. To not have your manhood questioned. So I shut the fuck up and laughed along and dapped them up after they bought me a lap dance from a woman named Cherry with a shaved head and a tattoo of a knife between her small breasts. I drank the shots of tequila they fed me and fed me, until I blacked out and woke up on the floor of the center's apartment living room. And then I signed the letter of intent a week later, committing to play there.

I must have finally fallen asleep around five thirty, because the last thing I remembered before Alaina shook me awake was the grey dawn framing her bedroom window and the mocking sound of birds chirping outside.

"Hey," she was saying. "Ty keeps calling you."

"What time is it?" I said. My eyes burned from lack of sleep, a feeling I'd get used too, that would soon become a sort of accomplice.

"Nine," Alaina said.

I sat up in bed, wiped the crust from the corner of my eyes. "I slept like shit."

"He's been texting you, too. Last one said, We got a problem."

Alaina handed me my phone. Five missed calls and two texts. Plus one from Dad that said, "U ok?" And another from somebody named Michael Pontecorvo from Channel 7 asking if I'd be available for a phone interview this afternoon. I had no idea how the fucker even got my number.

I tapped Ty's name in my contacts, put it on speaker. He answered before the second ring. Alaina handed me a mug of coffee stamped with a smiling bear and Asheville in cursive letters.

"Yo, bad news," Ty said.

I took a sip of the coffee, which Alaina had reheated in the microwave. It was scalding.

"Fuck."

"That's what I'm saying."

"Wait. What happened?"

"You didn't get an email?"

"Haven't checked." I blew the steam from the coffee, tested another sip.

"Check, bro."

I swiped out of the phone app, clicked my Gmail. Below an email from the same dickhead from Channel 7 was notice from Voyage Diagnostics. I swiped out of the email, afraid to read it in full.

"Piss test," I said.

"Bingo."

"Fuck," I said. Some of the coffee slushed over the edge of the mug and onto Alaina's white sheets. She rolled her eyes at me. I mouthed, *Sorry*. She left the room to get a rag. "Think it's just me and you?"

"Bishop knows we smoke."

"We all do."

"Yeah, but with us he can make a point."

"When?"

"Today. Before practice. And the Pharmacist? MIA. At the worst fucking time. He must be laying low. I kept telling him not to deal to frat boys."

"Where are we going to get clean piss in," I checked my email again, scanned the note, "like ninety minutes?"

Ty was quiet.

"Ty?"

"Alaina still with you?"

I took the call off speaker, held it to my head.

"No way," I said. I put the coffee down on the nightstand and kicked off the covers, stepped out of bed. Alaina came in with a damp rag and started dabbing the coffee stains on her sheets. She sucked air through her teeth, shot me daggers, then left the room again.

I lowered my voice.

"I can't ask her to do that."

"Why the fuck not?"

"Because this is our problem. I can't get her involved."

"It's about to be a big problem, bro. We can't get suspended. Not right now."

I squeezed the bridge of my nose. "Fuck."

Alaina appeared again in the doorway. Her annoyance had melted away into concern. I waved her impatiently away and instantly regretted it, but it was too late. She flipped me off and huffed out of sight. I went into the living room, didn't see Alaina, then went out through the sliding glass doors onto the little concrete landing where Alaina and her roommate had set up a rusty beach chair and a folding table. It was a cold, metallic morning. I was shirtless and in shorts. The parking lot was pebbled with rock salt. I shivered.

"It's just this one time," Ty reasoned. "Then never again."

"Fucking Bishop."

"I'm telling you."

"Can't even give us one night. After the shit we saw? I can't get Coach's face out of my brain, Ty. His eyes. I think trouble is coming for us. I barely slept last night."

I heard Ty exhale. "Right now we just need some piss."

Then he started laughing. So I did too. The kind of laughing that says, *I don't know how fucked up things are about to get, but we're gonna find out.*

"Let me talk to her," I said.

"Tell her it's for me if you have to."

"It won't be pretty."

"If you die, let me have your games."

"Is that all I am to you? An Xbox?"

"That and a wicked jumpshot."

"Say a prayer."

"In Kobe's name, Amen."

Alaina was waiting for me in the living room with her arms folded. I didn't stand a chance.

"What happened?" she said.

"Sit with me," I said.

I went to the couch, but she didn't follow, so I stood up again. I felt like an idiot.

"Bishop is planting his flag in the ground."

"What the fuck does that mean?"

"It means we have to take a piss test."

"You showed up blazed last night."

I shrugged. Alaina let her arms fall heavily at her sides.

"Fuck, Jason."

"Yeah."

"You and Ty?"

I nodded.

"*Fuck*, Jason. I mean, weed is basically legal here. What the fuck is his deal?"

"His deal is he went to West Point. Thinks he's a drill sergeant or some shit."

"Can you call that kid? The Doctor or whatever?"

I allowed a laugh.

"The Pharmacist. Ty can't get a hold of him."

"So, what are you going to do?"

I took a deep breath, let it out slowly, and the realization dawned on Alaina's face. She began shaking her head.

"No no no. I am not getting wrapped up in your fuckery." She turned her back on me and went into the kitchen. I followed.

"I didn't even say anything yet."

"Don't give me that bullshit, Jason. You were about to. You think I don't know you by now?"

"Well, my bullshit might prevent me, us, from making life-changing money. For me, you, my dad, your folks."

"Don't bring them into this." Alaina was pacing the kitchen, anxiously putting things away from the dishrack. I went up behind her and tried to hold her, but she squirmed free and turned and whacked me hard on the arm.

"Alaina," I said. I was pathetic and I knew it. "Just this once."

"No."

"Please."

"No!"

I had an idea. I went to the drawer by the fridge that held a scatter of random junk—batteries, instructions for the coffee machine, dead lighters— and took a rubber band, one of the thick blue ones that came from a thing of broccoli or whatever. When Alaina went to the cabinet, standing on her toes to put away a pair of pint glasses we stole from Mellow Mushroom, I dropped to one knee.

She turned and almost fell over me.

"Jesus. What the hell are you doing?"

"Look, I know this isn't the way you hoped it would go down—"

"Jason?"

"But listen. I love you so goddamn much, Alaina Payton. I love your smile, your energy, I love the way your neck looks when you wear your hair up, I love the way you smell when you haven't showered for two days and the way your fingers and toes look with the polish starting to chip off, I love your laugh—"

"Jason…"

"Listen, I love how you love me for me, the real me and all the chaos that comes with it. That's come with it since the beginning."

I started to get choked up and that was finally when Alaina realized I wasn't fucking around. She covered her mouth with her hands.

"Oh my God," she said. A whisper, almost to herself.

I held up the thick blue rubber band that I'd curled into a ring.

She snorted a laugh, wiped tears and snot with the cuff of her hoodie.

"I want to be with you forever, Alaina. No matter what happens. No matter if we live the life we dream about, or if it all comes crashing down. I know it'll be all good either way, because I'll have you by my side."

"Yes," she said and nodded. Her cheeks were slick and she looked as beautiful as I'd ever seen her.

"Alaina, will you marry me?"

"Yes. You fucking idiot, yes."

I put the rubber ring on her finger. It dangled loose, but it didn't matter. Alaina pulled me up off the tiled floor and kissed me long and hard.

"I promise as soon as I sign that contract, I'll get you the baddest ring you've ever seen."

"You better," Alaina said. She took the rubber band from off her finger and unspooled it and put it on her wrist. She whacked me hard on the arm again. "Asshole."

She sat on the toilet and spoke to me from behind the cracked door.

"How am I supposed to get it into this thing? I can't, like, aim like you can. Not that you really ever do."

"Can you squat over it?"

"Oh, wow, I hadn't thought of that. Thank God there's a man around to tell me how to pee."

"Can I help?" I started to push the door open.

"No! Jason! Do not come in here. Fuck, a little came out onto my foot."

"Gross."

"Fuck you, I cannot believe I said yes to this."

"I swear it's just this once."

"I mean marrying you, you dick."

"It took a long time to pick out that ring."

"I hate you so much. Make yourself useful and go get me a jar."

"A jar?"

"Yes, dummy. A jar. I can't pee straight into a Ziploc bag. We'll like, pour it in."

"I love you," I said. Then I went and did as I was told.

The trick, according to Reddit, was to keep the piss warm, right around body temp. Any warmer or cooler and they'd know me and Ty were tampering with it. Automatic fail. Automatic suspension. And then suddenly things don't look so pretty on the NBA draft board. Questions of character. Integrity. Which is bullshit, because like eighty percent of the NBA smokes weed, and it isn't even tested in the league anymore. And for Ty? Whatever small chance he had of hearing his name called would be out the window.

I took the Mason jar from Alaina, piss yellow as Mountain Dew, and microwaved it for thirty seconds. Then I put it into a pair of Ziploc freezer bags over the sink, one for me, one for Ty.

"You look like Walter White," Alaina said.

"You need to hydrate."

I ran the tap until the water got hot and used a thermometer until it read ninety-nine degrees. I filled a thermos halfway with the warm water, put the Ziploc bags in the thermos and screwed the lid.

"Here's to our future," I said.

Alaina chewed the inside of her cheek. She was nervous. I kissed her on the forehead.

"You seem calm," she said.

I shrugged. "When you don't sleep, maybe there's no energy for stress."

She brought me into a tight embrace. She still smelled like sleep.

"I love you, J. Even if you are an idiot."

"We'll be okay," I said.

Ty's truck was already in the parking lot, his rims rattling with the bass from his stereo. Alaina pulled up next to him. She looked at me, chewed the same spot on the inside of her cheek.

"It'll be fine," I said.

"This isn't normal, J."

"See you back at your place?"

She nodded. I leaned over the middle console of her Corolla, held her face in my hands and kissed her on the mouth.

I got out of the car, grabbed my bag from the backseat. As I did so, Ty rolled down his passenger window. Biggie spilled out.

"Alaina," he yelled.

She rolled down her window, waited for him to speak.

"We owe you one."

Alaina looked at him for a moment, deadpan, then rolled up her window and drove off.

"She pissed?" he said, as I climbed into his truck. He turned down the dial on the stereo. "No pun intended."

"Nah, she's happy we're about to use a thermos of her pee to sneak past a drug test. If we get caught, she could get fucked too, bro."

"This isn't a DNA test. They can't tell whose piss it is, long as it's clean."

I unzipped my gym bag and took out the thermos. I unscrewed the lid, took out the two Ziploc bags. Ty swatted at my arms. The runoff dripped onto my legs.

"Yo! Watch the seats!"

"Relax. It's water. To keep the bags warm."

Ty looked into the thermos. "Word?"

"Otherwise, they'll know."

"This is some *Ocean's Eleven* shit."

"You got the athletic tape?"

Ty popped the middle console, handed me the roll of soft white tape.

I took one of the Ziplocs and dried it on my sweatshirt.

"Damn, Alaina needs to drink more H2O."

"That's what I said."

I bit off a small piece of the tape, pulled down my sweats and taped the baggy to my inner thigh.

"Ugh," I said. "Warm."

"Mother*fuck*, Bishop," Ty said. "All for some tree."

I dried the other baggy, handed it over. Ty grimaced.

"Just do it," I said.

"Nike. How far are *you* willing to go to be great?"

He lowered his sweats, applied the tape.

"Like this?"

"Just make sure it's not going to fall off."

"After this bullshit, I'm going for a thirty piece against Tech."

"Let's pass first."

"If we don't? My life is over, bro. Seriously."

Ty looked at me. He was truly scared, as much as he tried to hide it behind loud music and loud talk.

"One step at a time," I said. I held out my fist. Ty exhaled, tapped it, cranked the volume knob for the last thirty seconds of "Things Done Changed."

Shea, our swing forward, was in the locker room when me and Ty got there. He was suiting up, putting on his practice jersey, compression tights and practice shorts. His phone was propped up on a shelf in his cubby playing a video. 21 Savage rapped with a cold-blooded stare.

"Need to get you some Biggie," Ty said. "Some Wu."

"Blahzey blah," Shea said. He barely glanced up from his phone. He wore his braids straight back like Carmelo did back in the day. He nodded toward the bathroom. "Kat's in there. Y'all get flagged?"

I didn't answer. Neither did Ty. That said everything Shea needed to know.

"Word," he said. "Good luck. We need y'all."

"We're not going anywhere," Ty said.

We had agreed I would go first because I'd read a whole mess of Subreddits about tips and tricks, do's and don'ts. In some ways, women had it easier, had the ability to sneak a Five Hour Energy bottle of clean piss in their vaginas. For men, it was a little more complicated. I read stories of guys who used prosthetic dicks to beat piss tests with their PO watching. Genius came in all shades.

Kat was sitting up on the long row of gleaming white and chrome sinks scrolling her phone, a box of opaque plastic cups by her thigh. Sixteen hours ago she was pounding on Coach's chest.

"Howdy," she said. Her short hair stuck up in the back as though she hadn't showered. The little diamond stud in her nose caught the light. In another life, one where I was a few years older and Kat didn't date women, I might've made a go. She put on a pair of fresh latex gloves, took a cup from the box and used a felt-tip marker to write my last name and the date on it. She handed it to me. "Pick a stall, any stall."

"You okay?" I said.

"Not really," she said with an ironic brightness. "But here we are."

"Here we are."

I took the last stall, farthest away from the sinks, and closed the door. I felt sweat trickle down my thigh and thanked god the tape held. I stuck my hand in my pants and lifted the toilet seat heavily so that it banged against the metal piping so I could take the bag off of my skin without making too much noise. It was still warm.

"Hey, Kat," I said.

"Talk to me."

"Can you run the sink? Too quiet in here."

"Jesus, Nichols. You can hit clutch free throws on the road against Miami, but you can't pee with a chick in the room?"

"Different ballgame."

This got a little laugh and then I heard the steady *shhh* of the sink.

"Appreciate you," I said. I broke the seal on the cup, unzipped the bag, and as carefully as I could, poured Alaina's bright yellow pee into the cup until it was three-quarters full. I tossed the rest, along with the Ziploc bag, into the toilet and flushed. I capped the cup as Kat shut the water off. I put down the seat, a habit chiseled into my brain from Mom, opened the door and went back to the sink where Kat took the cup with her gloved hands and put it into a cylindrical container with a temperature gauge on the lid.

"Thanks for doing business," Kate said. "I'd shake your hand, but you know. Maybe next time."

"Let's hope there is no next time," I said and ran my hands under the tap.

A few more of the guys were in the locker room when I returned. It was quiet, as though no one knew how to talk about what we'd been through. Shea was showing Malik and Corey, two of our freshmen, another 21 Savage video on his phone.

"Stop it," Shea said. "21 got way better visuals than Carti."

I could tell the freshmen disagreed but didn't dare say anything.

Ty was standing awkwardly at his locker, pretending to rearrange his boxes of Jordans.

"You're up, boss," I said, and nodded at him to let him know I'd pulled it off.

I watched Ty cross the locker room with a sort of waddling limp to keep the bag taped to his leg. When he was out of sight, I went to my locker and changed into my practice gear. I sat on my stool and scrolled my phone and waited. There was a text from Alaina:

???

I texted back, *I'm good. Waiting on Ty.*

There were three dancing bubbles, but they disappeared.

I didn't have to wait much longer. As I swiped out of my messages, Ty bounded back into the locker room with a grin like a little kid.

"My piss is like my jumper: cleannnnn."

I opened up my messages again: *We're good.*

I got a barf emoji in return.

Love you too, I wrote. Then I threw my phone in my bag.

We still had about twenty minutes until practice started, so I went into the gym to get some shots up in peace before Bishop charged in hot to announce the new regime. I already had a sweat going by the time Hunter, our team manager, a sports science major with chin-length stringy hair and glasses, started wheeling racks of balls onto the court.

"I'll feed you," he said.

I passed him the ball and then moved in an arc around the three-point line as he hit me with the sharpest chest passes he could manage. I hit fifteen threes in a row.

"Fuego," he said giddily as the last one, a corner three, my favorite spot on the court, spun through the net.

Somehow, despite an awful night's sleep, I felt sharp. Loose, as though my exhaustion meant my body and brain didn't have the capacity to carry tension. I could manage only the most essential functions, which in this case meant being deadly from three. Maybe sleep was overrated. Maybe that was the secret. Flow state. Muscle memory. Or maybe I was just beginning to crack.

"Don't wear yourself out, Nichols."

I heard Bishop's voice before I saw him emerge from the tunnel that led from the locker room. "I hope you brought your running shoes."

"Bring it," I shrugged.

The rest of the team and coaching staff filtered onto the court, and we gathered at center court around the circle that was inset in the giant outline of the state of Virginia. I caught Ty's eye across the circle. I winked at him. Banks looked like he'd barely slept. Shea had his hands on his hips. The assistant coaches, who had been Bishop's peers less than twenty-four hours ago, waited along with the rest of us for him to speak. I wondered what they were thinking, if they were willing to buy into his bullshit.

Bishop entered the middle of our circle in a pair of tapered sweats and a tucked-in team polo. It looked like he'd somehow found time to get a haircut. He wore a whistle around his neck and cradled a ball at his hip.

"Look," he said, "we're here because this is where Coach would want us to be, right?"

Half of us nodded.

"Some of you asked if we'd take a couple days off. NC State was pushed a week, but we've still got Tech on Sunday. So. If you need a few days? I won't stop you. We're all men here. But to me? We honor Coach by playing. By fighting. By working our FUCKING. ASSES. OFF." He bounced the ball hard on the court in between each word. "There will be time to mourn. Time to reflect. But right now? It's time to show this conference, this country, what we're made of. Now let's bring it in. Coach on three…"

What we were made of, it seemed, was a two-hour bootcamp. I hadn't run that hard since I was on high school varsity. Coach was out to prove a point, and the point was: *I'm going to run you fucks til you puke.* And that's exactly what happened. Practice started with suicides. Ten rounds of them. Then we moved on to seventeens, a sadistic drill that involves running sideline to sideline seventeen times in under a minute. The whole team. Which is goddamn impossible when you've got guys like Banks carrying two-hundred-ninety pounds around. And if you don't get seventeen in under a minute? You go again. And again. And again. Until you make it. But you never make it. That's the fucking point. You run until your legs are jelly and your vision turns to static and your ears start to ring and your chest is on fire and then Banks peels off mid-sprint to go barf in the corner, an unbelievable volume of yellowish-orange spew that lands on the court in a loud splat like creamed corn. And when we stopped running to half-gawk at him, half-look away, Coach screamed, "DID I BLOW THE GODDAMN WHISTLE? Start over." So we did. And when I looked at Coach, I swear to god he was smiling. The sick fuck.

"There you go, Banks. Get it all out. You need to shed a few anyway. Cut back on the lasagna at team meals, Big Boy."

I started to wonder if all this running might have burned the THC out of me and Ty's blood the old-fashioned way.

Eventually, Bishop took some kind of pity on us. We were barely hitting seventeen in ninety seconds, let alone sixty. All fifteen of us, twelve scholarship guys and three walk-ons, were doubled over, grabbing the hem of our shorts, sweat pooling at our feet.

"Thinks he's that motherfucker from *Whiplash*," Ty whispered to me.

"You got something to share, Gilchrist?" Bishop said. He whipped a chest pass at Ty and Ty reacted quick enough to catch it.

"Yeah, I do," Ty said with an edge.

"Chill," I said under my breath.

"I said you think you're the big bad boss now. Got us puking, on the verge of blacking out. The fuck is this? Our coach *died*, bro."

Bishop smirked. I knew he was an asshole, but this was turning into something different.

"*I'm* your coach now, Tyson. You want to take the rest of the day off? Be my guest." He stepped to the side and held out his arm like a matador. "The rest of us will be focused on turning this ship around.

We lost three and a row and it would've been four. You like to lose?"

"Nah."

"What?"

"NAH!"

"That's what I thought. So show me. Or get the fuck off my team."

Ty fired a pass right back at Coach. Coach caught it, smirked again.

"Good," he said.

Next was War. We paired off two by two, dove on the floor to fight for the ball that Bishop rolled out in front of us. If he was concerned at all about us getting hurt, he didn't show it. Conference play was about to heat up, our toughest stretch of the season, and he had us out there like it was a tryout. Of course, I got paired up with Malik, a freshman swing-forward, six-six, thin as a pencil, razorblade elbows, and when we dove on the floor after the ball, I caught one of those elbows right in the cheekbone. Malik came away with the ball and I came away with a gash under my left eye that immediately leaked blood all down my face, off my chin, and into little ruby puddles on the court. It tasted bright and metallic on my tongue and reminded me of the time as a kid when I took a charge during a summer rec league game and my bottom teeth went right through my lip. Mom was at the game, one of the few she was able to catch, and she brought me over to the water

fountain to rinse my mouth out. I didn't cry because
my teammates were looking. When the water came
straight out through the hole, she said, "Toughness
has nothing to do with tears."

Coach blew the whistle so Hunter could come
out and wipe the blood off the floor, and Kat could
clean up my cut, smudge some Vaseline on it and
apply a butterfly bandage to stop the bleeding.

"Stitches?" I said.

"I think you're good," she said. "The face
bleeds a lot, but it's not that deep by the looks of it."

"You're supposed to say yes and get me out of
this shit."

She smiled. "Sorry, kid. You're on your own."

"Nothing wrong with a little blood, Nichols,"
Coach said. "What'd I say? This is war. In war, blood
gets spilled, don't it?"

We finished practice with cutthroat. Full
court. Three-on-three. The only way to win? Get
three stops in a row on defense. If not? Fifty push-ups
and you get your asses to the back of the line to try
again.

It was me, Malik, and Corey, the other
freshmen, five-eleven and a hundred-fifty pounds
soaking wet. Coach knew what he was doing. Testing
me. Seeing if I would bitch. If I would break. Trying
to get me to flip out on him so he had an excuse to
tell me I'd never make it at the next level with a
bullshit attitude. But by then I was so gassed from

lack of sleep and our wicked practice that I didn't give a fuck. I was winning no matter who he put me with. It took us four tries. Four trips on and off the floor. Four full sprints up and down the court. A hundred-fifty push-ups, until our arms were rubbery noodles. But we did it. Our final stop was against Ty and Banks and a seven-foot walk-on named Ethan who had the coordination of a drunk giraffe. Ty came right at me and tried to hit me with a double crossover, but I knew him so well by then that I could feel it coming and cut him off, beat him to his spot and he dribbled the ball off his foot and out of bounds. I screamed up toward the rafters as Coach blew his whistle and we all collapsed to the floor, completely drained.

"Lucky bitch," Ty said.

"Welcome to the Terrordome," Bishop said. Then he smiled.

Our game at home against NC State was postponed. The funeral was held at St. Stephens, a church on the north side of campus. I hadn't been inside a church since Mom died, and as I sat there and listened to the priest, a paunchy fifty-something with a pale face and black framed glasses, drone on about the many treasures of the kingdom, I remembered why. Churches creeped me the fuck out. The cold wood benches. The emaciated dead man hanging in agony from a cross. The incense, stale and ancient. And the cult-like energy: the sitting and standing on cue, the chanted prayers, the horror movie organ, all of it. I tried to remind myself that this was for Coach, but I had a hard time picturing him in a space like this. He was too kinetic. Too alive. It was almost impossible to believe his body was laying in the polished wood casket at the foot of the altar. Especially because the lid was closed, just like Mom's had been.

He would've been blown away though, because the church was packed out. We all sat front right, first three rows, along with the coaches, staff, wives, and girlfriends. Coach's family, which was really just his two sisters and their husbands and kids, sat across the aisle and cried softly throughout the service. Behind us, the rows were full of the major faces of college athletics, our school and beyond. School president, athletic director, coaches from the other athletic programs, alumni, boosters, former players—including a couple of current and former NBA guys—coaches from other schools, and way in the back, a woman from ESPN who Coach respected and who had written about him a few times over the years. It was beautiful to see, and I wished Coach would've had a chance to get his flowers while he was still alive to smell them.

A half-dozen people went up to the podium to pay their respects. As the captain, I was voted to represent the team. Forty-eight hours ago, I was walking around with a bag of piss taped to my leg. Now I was about to go up and represent our team in front of a who's who of our sport. Coach's older sister, a woman with a dark bob of hair named Moira, went up first. The church was silent as she dabbed her eyes with a tattered ball of tissue and tried to compose herself.

"Excuse me," she sniffed. The podium mic crackled as she shuffled a sheaf of handwritten looseleaf. Alaina squeezed my hand. It was easy to forget that Coach was a real person with a real life outside the game, small as it was.

"Calvin was my younger brother," she began. "Believe it or not, he used to look up to me. He listened to me. I'm sure it's hard to imagine him listening to anyone, but it's true. There was a park down the street from our apartment in Brooklyn, and when my parents needed some peace and quiet, I would take him down there to play. He'd ride this little red tricycle and wear one of those toy football helmets, you know, with the single bar? Except the thing was way too big, so it would slide down over his eyes. People in the neighborhood loved it. Loved him." She sniffled again. "Excuse me." She wiped her nose. "Cars would slow down. Honk. People pointing and waving. He'd wave back. Then ride around the blacktop like a little madman. His face getting all pink. I'd chase him around. He'd squeal with delight. I can still hear it. It was fun. Despite our difference in age, we were friends. But one day, I'm telling you, everything changed. One day, a high school boy was in the park with a basketball. There wasn't even a goal, but he was working on his dribbling. Doing drills, up and down, up and down. Calvin was mesmerized by that orange ball. He got up off his little tricycle and went over and just watched. Eventually, the boy noticed and rolled the ball to Calvin. I knew right then: love at first sight. I wish I could explain the look on his face to you. It was—" Her voice wavered and broke. She covered her face. Her shoulders shook. Alaina clucked her tongue sympathetically, squeezed my hand harder, leaned against me and put her other hand on my forearm.

"Sorry," Coach's sister said. She dabbed her eyes with the back of her wrist. "Look what you made me do, you little shit," she said in the direction of the casket. This drew a gentle laugh from the assembly.

"Anyway, you know where this is going. Basketball. The love of my brother's life. He would have coached regardless of the level. And as many of you know, this game gives a lot, but it can take a lot too. Sometimes I wonder if I'd never brought Calvin to the park that day…if…" she trailed off. "But then I catch myself. No. Because the game would have found him. And the game is better *because* of him. He touched a lot of young men's lives." She looked in our direction, scanned for eye contact, for a moment settling on mine. "He loved you boys. He loved to teach. To lead. He loved this community, the joy it brought to the fans. And he hated to lose. Boy did he hate it. Especially that Podunk school down the road." This drew a genuine laugh that took a second to subside. She looked again at us players. "Make him proud with the rest of the season. Play like he would want you to play. Play hard. Have fun. Try to love the game and each other like he loved the game and he loved you." She turned her gaze on the casket. "I love you Calvin. We all do." Then she folded up her paper, stepped down from the podium and joined the rest of her family in the row across the aisle. She fell into her younger sister's arms and sobbed.

After a respectful amount of time had passed, the Athletic Director, a trim Black man in a smart black suit and frameless glasses, went up to the podium. He had played baseball at the school in the nineties, a speedy outfielder who had brought us to the brink of a college World Series title. He cleared his throat and spoke in a steady, measured voice about Coach's integrity, his passion, his hard-headed stubbornness. His deep love for the university. His impact on the community, his commitment to giving back, including the times where Coach dragged him out to the parking lot of Harris Teeter dressed as an ebony and ivory pair of Santas and rang the bell for Salvation Army. He was a great Coach, an even better man, and he would be missed. The AD ended by saying that a banner would be raised in the arena in his name, his signature stenciled on the court, black bands affixed to our jerseys, and the remainder of all active athletic seasons dedicated in his honor.

It only felt appropriate to clap for these pronouncements, so we did. We stood and clapped as the AD left the podium and I stayed standing because it was my turn to go up.

"Just be you," Alaina said, and kissed my cheek.

I went up and looked out at the faces, chins tipped, expectant. All that black fabric. I hadn't written anything down because I knew exactly what I wanted to say. The trouble was, I'd slept about eight hours total in the last seventy-two. My brain was fuzzy and slow. My nerves were starting to fray. I looked at Coach Bishop, his thin lips a hyphen, and I knew all he was thinking about was power and control. The opposite of Coach.

"On my official recruiting visit," I said, "Coach took me to the arena. They dimmed the lights. They had Jeff Anderson record a player intro for me. That booming voice: *a six-five guard, number eleven, Jason Nichols.* I still get goosebumps. And yeah, all the theatrics were cool. But when Coach handed me a jersey with my name stitched over number eleven, it was what he said to me that I'll remember forever: *I know how much that number means to you.*" The memory brought a lump to my throat. I tried to swallow it back. I looked at Alaina and she nodded like, *You got this.*

"That's who he was. He cared about us as hoopers, but more importantly, he cared about *us.* Always asking about our families, checking in on us, bringing us into his office to have real conversations, as men. I mean, there was hardly anywhere to sit because of all the boxes of old game film and scouting reports and diet Dr. Pepper," there was a muttering of laughter, "but he treated us with respect, spoke to us as the men we hoped to become. If I regret anything? It's that for all the times he checked in on me, I wish I'd taken the time to check in on him." I cleared my throat, that damn lump again. To compose myself, I tilted my head back and looked to the ceiling, the wood beams, the wrought-iron light fixtures. Mistake. Everything was wavy. Quivering. A prickle of heat whispered at my neck. A shadowy white pulse edged my vision. I felt my pulse thump beneath my collar.

I was starting to panic.

Not here.

Not now.

"If you're up there Coach?" My hands went ice cold. "We love you, we miss you, and we dedicate the rest of the season to you."

And maybe I'd ruptured my delicate equilibrium when I tilted my head back. Maybe my nerves weren't built for such a naked display of vulnerability. But as I leveled my gaze to the looming blank faces, my legs wobbled, the room lurched on its axis, my vision went black, and I collapsed in a heap to the hard marble floor.

I came to briefly in the back of Ty's truck. Alaina was sitting next to me holding a gym towel to the back of my head. She was, or had been, crying. I met Ty's eyes in the rearview mirror as he braked at a stoplight. We were on the way to the university hospital.

"You really stole the show back there, Champ."

"What happened?"

"You fell down go boom," Ty said.

The light turned green, and he gunned it off the line. My head snapped back against the middle headrest.

"Jesus, Ty," Alaina said.

"My bad."

"How bad is it?"

"You've got a nice little gash. Your head smacked the ground pretty hard. Nice echo in that church."

"Shit sounded like a coconut," Ty said.

"You scared the hell out of me," Alaina said. "All of us."

"Except Bishop. He barely moved when we all went to pick you up."

"I don't know what happened," I lied. "I was feeling fine."

Alaina took the gym towel from behind my head to fold it in quarters, finding a clean side. At the sight of the fresh blood, a deep crimson Rorschach test, I passed out again.

The next time I opened my eyes, I was seated at an angle in an examination chair. Drape-like partitions were pulled shut around the room and a fluorescent light burned overhead. I still had my suit pants and shoes on, but my jacket and dress shirt were removed. Alaina sat in a chair next to me, tapping at her phone.

"Where's Ty?" I said.

Alaina looked at me and said, "You keep asking that. You don't remember? They only let one person back here with you, so he went back to the service to let everyone know you're okay and in good hands."

"Am I okay?"

At that moment, a doctor in a white coat pulled aside the curtain and came in with a nurse in purple scrubs carrying a steel tray with a needle and stitches.

"Mr. Nichols," the doctor said, brightly, "Welcome back." His nameplate said Dr. Philippoussis and he had a big bulbous nose and horseshoe of black hair. An archipelago of purple birthmarks scattered across his pate. "This is Nurse Ryan. She's going to get you stitched up and back to hitting jumpers."

"Was I awake when I got here?"

"Intermittently. Not unusual for a concussion."

"Concussion?"

"Mm. You're lucky that's all it is. Scans and X-Rays all look fine, but we'd like to check your noggin again when those stitches come out to be absolutely certain."

The young woman, a graduate nurse, I figured, had her blonde hair pulled tight into a braid. Her blue eyes were alert behind electric blue eyeglasses. She came to the side of my chair and prepped the needle, stuck it into a little jar of clear liquid.

"The good stuff?"

"Local anesthetic," she said. "So you don't feel me poking around with the stitches. Fair warning, I'm going to have to shave a little spot of your hair."

"Just make sure I look tough," I said. I looked at Alaina and she rolled her eyes. She was feeling better.

"You'll feel a little pinch. Then it might start to feel cold. That means it's working."

I winced a bit at the sharp stab near the wound, then felt a cold burning sensation as the liquid leaked beneath my scalp.

"Feel that?"

I could tell she was shaving a patch of my hair, but I didn't feel a thing. I shook my head.

"Perfect."

"I'm sorry about Coach Reynolds," Dr. Philippoussis said. "What a shame. I met him once at Homestead Steakhouse. He was there with a few of friends. My wife begged me not to bother him, but I stopped at his table on the way out. He shook my hand. Couldn't have been nicer."

"That's who he was," I said. But I was thrown by the word *friends*. There were sides to Coach that I'd never know, and this reality made me enormously sad.

"University red," Nurse Ryan said. In her palm, she held a little spool of blood-red thread.

"Can't have you out there looking like a chump," the doctor said.

"Too late," Alaina said.

"When can I play?" I said.

"You should be good in about a week. Just make sure you take care of the wound and get some rest. Which, have you been having trouble sleeping?"

"Why?"

"Well, when you were coming in and out, you were telling us how tired you've been."

"It's been a long few days."

The doctor nodded. "With a concussion, especially the first night, we'll need you," he nodded at Alaina, "to wake him up every few hours just to make sure he's lucid."

"All done," Nurse Ryan said. She snipped the last of the thread. "Want to see?"

Alaina got up and took a look.

"Gnarly," she said.

The nurse took a picture with her phone and showed me. I had a quarter-sized bald spot and a little line of stitches puckering my skin. Tiny beads of black blood tried to squeeze through.

"Tough," I said.

"They're waterproof, so you can shower and all that. Just don't hit the gym for a few days. So that jumper might get a little rusty." Dr. Philippoussis winked.

"Never."

"Good, cause we're gonna need it. You guys gotta get off the bubble and into the Tourney, my friend. Speaking of which, my son is a huge fan. Would you mind?"

He handed me a pen and a prescription pad, so I scrawled my messy signature and #11 right where the name of the drugs would go.

Alaina didn't need to worry about waking me up throughout the night, because I still couldn't sleep. We got in bed together, but I knew right away. It was hopeless. My brain was on. A distant chatter in the back of my head, a radio station stuck at low volume. Alaina quickly fell asleep on my chest, so I gently rolled her over, turned off the alarms she'd set to check on me, and went to the living room with my laptop. To keep from thinking about Coach's empty dead eyes, his sister and her deep well of sorrow, about Ty and the piss test, about Dr. Philippoussis and the cluelessness of his autograph hunting, I pulled up YouTube, searched for Mom, and there she was. Washington Mystics, number 11. The pure jump shot, fluid and pretty. The near constant movement without the ball, making cuts, coming off screens, anything to get open, to get the ball, to do the one thing she was born to do: shoot. I watched her hit six threes against Rebecca Lobo and the New York Liberty. A corner three game-winner against the Phoenix Mercury, her stone-cold reaction as her teammates went berserk around her and toppled onto the floor.

I watched as the clock on my laptop swept past one. Two. Three. Four. Until it was time to take the extra-strength pain medication to keep the throbbing in my skull at bay. Four-thirty. Five. Until the birds began their chattering mockery on the other side of the window. Until my brain must have reached capacity and I awoke to Alaina shaking my shoulder and saying, "What the fuck, Jason," the computer still on my lap, my legs outstretched on the coffee table, pure pins and needles, and Mom, now a little older and with shorter hair, hit a teammate with a pinpoint behind-the-back pass on a fast break.

"Couldn't sleep."

"How long have you been out here?"

I rubbed my temples.

"All night."

She nudged me over and sat down next to me on the couch. She pulled her oversized t-shirt over her knees. She looked at what I'd been watching.

"Baby."

I said nothing.

"Let me see it."

I tilted my head. She sucked air through her teeth.

"It looks kind of like a squashed blueberry."

"I think something is wrong with my head."

"Yeah, it bounced off a 19th century Italian marble floor."

"No, like…I've never had trouble falling asleep this many nights in a row. And never like, almost the entire night."

Alaina hugged her knees to her chest.

"It makes sense though, right? You literally watched your coach, who you loved, who loved you, die right in front of you. In the middle of a game. In front of like, ten thousand people."

"Twelve."

"You know what I'm saying."

She reached over and shut my laptop right as Mom hit a corner three. Her favorite spot too.

"That's some traumatic shit, Jason. I watched you *pass out*. Your eyes rolled up in your skull. It was scary."

I nodded. My head throbbed. I was exhausted, but somehow wired at the same time. Like my brain was so tired it had made a full revolution around to alertness again. Still, there was a shadow of fatigue trailing my every thought and movement like a ghost.

"I feel like I can't turn my brain off. Like my thoughts are a drip from a busted faucet."

"Well at least we know your brain is on."

She was trying to keep it light. I couldn't blame her, but I couldn't meet her there. Everything felt so heavy.

"Give yourself some grace, okay? That's what Beth tells me all the time in therapy. You witnessed something horrible. And then, you know, the stress of the whole pee thing."

"You sure you want to marry a crazy person?"

"You're not going crazy, Jason. And yes, my entire family is batshit, so welcome to the squad."

She leaned against me and I hugged her close.

"Practice today?"

"Weights and film. Just film for me though. Bishop is going to love that."

"I hate him already."

"Welcome to the squad."

"Ty picking you up?"

I checked my phone. A text from Ty: *OMW you good?*

I liked the text, put my phone down and ran my hand up underneath Alaina's t-shirt, feeling the smooth legs and the little hairs in between.

"Don't start something you can't finish," she said. "Wouldn't want those stitches to pop out."

She pushed her legs out from under her t-shirt and stood up from the couch.

"Don't look at me like that, Tired Boy. I'll be here when you get back. Things will get back to normal. Promise."

Coach had to holler to be heard over the booming thump and knock of hip hop thundering from the speakers in the weight room.

I was spotting Ty at the bench since I couldn't do any lifting myself. This after I put my stitches on display for the guys to gawk and wince at in the locker room.

The clank and clatter of weights and metal and Bishop yelling our names.

"Gilchrist! Nichols! Come see me!"

Ty's eyes met mine upside down from where he lay on the bench press. He let the bar fall heavy on the stanchion with a clank.

"We're good," I said.

Ty took a clean towel from the stack by the door and wiped the sweat from his face, neck, and arms as we went down the sleek carpeted hallway from the weight room to Bishop's office. He took the durag off his braids and put it in the pocket of his warm-up pants.

"Maybe it's about Tech. You're sitting, so maybe I'm gonna move to the two."

"Could be," I said.

Bishop's door was half-open, so I knocked on the jamb. His name had already replaced Coach's on the placard.

"Yeah," Bishop said.

I pushed open the door and we went in. Bishop was sitting on a brown leather couch with socked feet up on a black marble coffee table. He pressed pause on a remote and the game film on the flat screen mounted on the opposite wall froze. Our last game. The first half. Before Coach dropped dead.

"Take a seat," Bishop said. He motioned to the two wing chairs facing the couch.

Coach's stuff had already been cleaned out. The walls were blank and there were cardboard bankers boxes stacked around the office. Scouting reports, recruiting magazines, plaques, photos. The ephemera of the coaching life.

I didn't like the look on Bishop's face. He looked smug. Like he knew he had the winning hand. The heat of hatred climbed my neck.

"I've got good news for you gentlemen," he said.

I felt Ty glance at me from my periphery.

Bishop set his feet down off the coffee table. He leaned over and took a red folder with our logo stamped on it from a stack of them set next to a fake succulent in a white pot. He opened the folder and took out two sheets of paper. He handed one to me and one to Ty. It was a printout of bio levels and hormones. My name was up top beneath the logo for Voyage Diagnostics.

"What's this?" I said.

"I wondered the same thing myself," Bishop said. "Matter of fact, when Kat told me, I had her reach out to double check."

I scanned the levels for clues. Glucose. Hemoglobin. Biotin. Names that meant nothing to me. It was clear we had failed. What wasn't clear was how. Next to me, Ty was silent, but his knee was pumping up and down.

"Allow me to be the first to say congratulations," Bishop said. He clasped his palms together. "You're both pregnant."

"Bullshit," Ty said, forcing a laugh.

The blood drained from my face. I shivered.

"As if this team isn't going through enough." Bishop's tone hardened. "Although… shit, if this is one of your little girlfriend's or whatever, you got bigger fish to fry."

I swallowed. My throat was gravel.

"What does this mean?" I managed to say. My voice was brittle.

"It means that in nine months, a baby will enter this clown show of a world we live in, Nichols."

"But like, for us?"

"Well that's an easy one, isn't it? You're both suspended. Indefinitely."

Ty sprang from his chair.

"Yo! Coach!"

"*Ty*. Sit down, son. And shut the fuck up."

"We watched our coach die," I said to no one in particular. The words and numbers on the sheet of paper were a blurry soup. How was I going to tell Alaina? And when?

"A tragedy," Bishop said. "But that doesn't excuse your towering idiocy. You have a responsibility. As men. As members of this team. As students of this university, which, I'll add, pays for your stupid asses to be here. And you failed to uphold that responsibility. Actions have consequences."

"It's weed, Coach," Ty said.

I shot him a look. As if it even mattered at this point.

"Please don't suspend me. There's only like, five games left. And my mom…" He trailed off. I knew him enough to know he was on the verge of crying.

Bishop's face lost its edge. Barely.

"What would you do in my position?"

I didn't have an answer. Neither did Ty.

"You can't win without us," I said. A mistake. I knew it as soon as the words left my mouth. Bishop's face hardened again.

"Oh no?" He leaned over, elbows on knees, closing the gap between us. A snarl curled his lips.

"Jay," Ty said.

"Watch me," Bishop said.

But I was too busy watching myself, as though from above. Watching it all unravel. A scared twenty-one-year-old with no real skills beyond what he could do with a basketball, a kid with no mother, an absent father, a future teetering on the brink. So, all I could do was laugh. Laugh despite the stricken look on Ty's face, the confusion on Bishop's, because if there was one thing I knew, it was that it would all be over for certain if I cried.

Acknowledgements

A million thanks to Scott Bolohan and .406 Press for the belief and support. Means so much.

Thank you to Jared Hedges for the killer cover design.

Thank you to John Brandon, Emily Costa, and Eric Rasmussen for your words and your kindness.

Thank you to Penny and Shawn and Alonzo and AI and Rickey and Ken and Kenny.

Thank you to Mom, Dad, Shannon, and Danicah. Love You.

Early versions of some stories appeared in the following places:

"Headhunter" in *Words & Sports Quarterly*
"Lunchbreak" in *Sundog Lit*
"Invaders" in *New Delta Review*
"Big Phipps Climbs the High Dive" in *Taco Bell Quarterly*
"Hang Time," "Beanball," and "There's No Such Thing as a Lil Life" in the *Under Review*
"Rickey Henderson Sits by a Lake" in *The Twin Bill*
"Tully" in *Molotov Cocktail*
"Wishbones" in *Coffin Bell*
"If You're Not First You're Last" in Reckon Review
"They Played Enya at the Monster Truck Rally" in *Maudlin House*
"Drop Zone" in *Farewell Transmissions*
"What Gouda Knew" in *jmww*

About the Author

Brendan Gillen is the author of *Static*. His short stories have been nominated for the Pushcart Prize and Best Small Fictions. He lives in Brooklyn. You can find him online at bgillen.com and on X/IG @beegillen.

www.ingramcontent.com/pod-product-compliance
Lightning Source LLC
Chambersburg PA
CBHW031530310726
48971CB00008B/2426